Sexton Blake:

The Missing Millionaire

by

Joseph A. Lovece

Based on the novel by Harold Blyth

Dime Novel Cover Vol. 7

ISBN-13: 978-1503284876
ISBN-10: 1503284875

Also by the author:

The Steam Man of the West
The Road Home
The Flying Prairie Schooner
The Transatlantic Race

Dime Novel Cover:

Denver Doll the Detective Queen
Six Weeks in the Moon
Hank Hound, the Crescent City Detective
Sherlock Holmes Versus Jack the Ripper
Hercules, the Dumb Destroyer
Night Hawk

TABLE OF CONTENTS

Introduction

The story of Sexton Blake begins with a whimper, not a
bang. And that's not from lack of trying. The character's name
first appeared in print in an Editor's Page in Alfred Harmsworth's new story paper *Halfpenny Marvel* No. 5, December 9,
1893:

"On this page we will be able to introduce you to three
of the characters who will figure very prominently in our next
number. In the early part of the next story a millionaire mys-
teriously disappears, and Sexton Blake, a very clever and daring
detective, takes the case in hand, determined that his investigations shall bring froth fruit...We will not enter into the details
of the plot—which is a very fascinating one—as to do so would
only anticipate the readers' interest...Without fear of
contraction, we say that it will be read by all with unflagging
interest from the first line to the last."

1

His readers seemed to agree. In *Halfpenny Marvel* No. 12, January 27, 1894, the editor said that according to the letters it received one of the two best stories to appear in the magazine was "The Missing Millionaire".

As promised the story appeared in *Halfpenny Marvel* No. 6, December 16, 1893, with a sequel the following issue. The problem was that the creator, Harold Blyth (1852-1898), writing under the pen name Hal Merideth, was a hack. According to the Website British Comics Miscellany, Blyth's stories are "border-line-unreadable. The plots rely on ridiculous coincidences, things that happen with no explanation (things often blow up if it's convenient!), and people magically knowing about/forgetting things when they need to."

Indeed, "The Missing Millionaire" is no exception. The coincidences are egregious, plot holes abound and Blake's judgment is questionable. It is no mystery, then, that the story opens up with him brooding over his lack of paying clients. Blyth wrote a handful of such stories before he died from typhoid a few years later. When more capable hands took over the character it eventually rose to stardom, and would be called "the poor man's Sherlock Holmes." More than 4,000 of his stories exist, penned by more than 200 authors, plus movies, radio serials, comic books and a television series. Sexton Blake became an important literary figure in spite of Blyth, not because of him.

Regarding the character's origin, Jess Nevins notes that

Harmsworth liked a series Blyth wrote on London crimes and hired him to write detective stories. The tale behind selection of Sexton Blake's first name is in dispute, with Blyth's sons claiming to have picked it, and former Harmsworth editors saying the 18-year old magazine's editor Somers J. Summers or the publisher himself was responsible. The last name Blake is credited to be a reference to a popular American dime novel sleuth, Jackson Blake.

The story is rewritten here not because of its quality, but because of its historical significance. In addition, the first novel has been transcribed from the original source character-for-character so the reader may compare them if he is so inclined.

The Missing Millionaire

by

Joseph A. Lovece

Chapter I

The detective leaned back on a divan, smoked a
cigarette, and considered fate. His serious face was clean-shaven
and his nose hawkish. He was tall and hard and ready for action.
He wondered when luck would go his way. People seemed to
attract like: bad luck begat more and good luck showered. Until
it didn't. He offhandedly mused that luck was a virus. His bad
streak would soon end—he could feel it. And it was about time.
He considered himself one of London's most clever detectives
and a scrapper few could beat. Sexton Blake was like the
detectives of old, smart and skilled but brave and active. He
found great traction in using disguises, and acting. So far his

6

skills were worth a bare living and a shabby office.

There was a knock at the door and a man stuck in his head.

"Mr. Frank Ellaby wishes to see you, sir."

"Good!" answered Blake. "Send him up, and at once."

The clerk withdrew and his master gazed at the grimy window of his New Inn Chambers office.

"So," he muttered, "my rich client has come at last, thanks to Gervaise. I wonder what it could be that pays so well? He said it may keep me busy for a year or two."

The door again opened, and a tall, handsome man, with cheeks bronzed by travel and having large and prominent grey eyes entered.

"You are Mr. Blake?" he said, as he paused on the threshold.

"Very much at your service, Mr. Ellaby. Pray take a seat and tell me your story. Mr. Gervaise told me to expect you, but little else."

"It will prove more troublesome than dangerous," said the visitor with a slight smile. "I'll tell you my tale and then you'll understand exactly what I want.

"My sister and I were orphans before we finished our schooling. She followed some friends to Australia, where I believe she obtained a comfortable living. You don't need to know how I survived then. When I was about twenty I, like thousands of other men, old and young, had a severe attack of

7

gold fever. I was determined to get to the Antipodes by hook or by crook, and try my luck at the diggings. If I came across my sister well and good; although I did not start with any plan to find her. I had one object in view, and one only—wealth!

"I am successful," he added, with a heavy sigh, "but my heart is empty, and my life has no meaning!

"In Australia I met a man and his wife with whom I became so friendly that he and I became partners in a claim. We toiled at it for months without finding one grain of gold. He was some years older than me, and he went by the name of Calder Dulk. I don't suppose that was his real name, but I didn't know then he was a liar.

"In those days I would have trusted him with my life. He was younger than his wife who was a tall, majestic woman of French extraction, wonderfully accomplished, fiercely ambitious and completely unscrupulous.

"I always mistrusted her and, unfortunately, I couldn't conceal my dislike.

"Just when we were despairing of ever having any luck, and were thinking of seeking our fortune in some other part, we struck a rich vein of precious ore, and found ourselves wealthy.

"Like many before us, this sudden success turned our heads. Nothing would do but we must hasten to Melbourne and celebrate.

"A few days after we arrived there I accidentally found the house where my sister lived. I got there just in time to bid her goodbye forever. She was dying. A beautiful, golden haired girl of perhaps four years of age was playing in the room.

"'Frank' she gasped, 'I swore to little Rose's mother, when *she* lay on *her* deathbed, that I would protect her child until she came of age. Swear it to me, Frank, so that I may die in peace.'

"There was, of course, no refusing this request at that awful moment, so I most solemnly took the vow she wished.

"My sister directed me to a cabinet which she said contained papers explaining who Rose's parents were. 'When you read them you'll understand how important she is, and that she must be guarded until she becomes an adult.' She didn't just tell me, which I found rather annoying.

"As she ceased speaking, she pressed my hand in hers. Smiling at me, she passed on to join the choir invisible.

"This event so distressed me that I could do nothing in connection with the child or anything just then. Calder Dulk led me away from the place to the hotel where we were staying. He advised me to remain alone and keep quiet until the next day, which I did.

"By the next morning both he and his wife had disappeared, and they had taken every ounce of gold I possessed. And that's not all. They had taken the child, too, and the papers."

"What was in the papers?" said Blake.

"I never looked at them. I don't need to tell you how hard that blow struck me, my reversal of fortune, the betrayal and my inability to keep my oath.

"I couldn't follow them; I had no money, not even to pay the hotel bill. All I could do was return to the diggings and try again."

"What about the hotel bill?"

"What?"

"You said you couldn't pay the hotel bill. What did you do?"

"Really? That's what you want to know? I signed an I.O.U. to the manager. I explained my situation, and being a gentleman and a humanitarian, he extended credit to me. Of course, his collectors were unsympathetic men, but I had some time to settle.

"As I was saying, there was nothing I could do but return to the diggings, and by hard labour again woo the goddess of chance's favor.

"I swore then in my heart that if I ever did attain wealth I would spend every farthing of it hunting down the traitor, and finding the child stolen from me! So, Mr. Sexton Blake, I am here to obtain your cooperation in this search, which must never cease till my end is attained!"

"How long is it since this double robbery was committed?" asked the detective.

"A sensible question. Fourteen years."

"Oof! That's a long time. Dulk and his wife may be dead; the girl has become a woman—"

"And a beautiful one, too, I am sure. You see," Ellaby explained, "for a long time my luck was so bad I scarcely succeeded in keeping body and soul together. \

"I hear you," said Blake.

" BILL BENDER SEIZED A HEAVY CUT-GLASS WATER BOTTLE WHICH WAS NEAR AT HAND, AND RAISING IT HIGH ABOVE HIS HEAD CRIED: 'MOVE A STEP AND I'LL BRAIN YOU.' "

"What?"

"Nothing. Go on."

"It is only recently that the wheel of fortune has taken a turn. Then, as always happens, gold poured in on me till I was

11

tired of gathering it."

"How terrible for you," Blake mused. "Have you heard anything of these people since?"

"Absolutely nothing. But your Parisian friend Gervaise claims that Madame Dulk visited the capital recently. While there she plundered the aristocracy in a grand, daring and shameless fashion. But no one answering her husband's description was seen visiting her. As she has reportedly left France we surmise that she is either in England or America."

"A very wide address," said Blake, with a smile. "If she is a high-toned adventuress, and is in London, she'll be easily found. But you're giving me a tall order. When Stanley was sent to Africa to find Livingston his search was at least limited to one continent. The whole world is before me. But I will do my best."

"Do that, and whether you fail or succeed, you shall have your own reward. Day and night I shall be at your service to aid you, and you may direct me as you choose."

"We'll work together, and I can promise you my complete attention. But I'm afraid that if we find Calder Dulk I'll have helped to being about a murder."

"What do you mean?" demanded Ellaby.

"Just this: you wish to meet him so that you may kill him!"

"When I get him there will be time enough for me to decide what I'll do with him," replied the millionaire. "I know you can't give me any useful advice off-hand. I must let you have a little time to digest my story. Meanwhile, will you lunch with me? I have been away from England so long that it will be safer for both of us if I trust to you to select the restaurant."

"With pleasure," said Blake. "Let's stroll over to Charing Cross. I think best when I'm walking. Come round this way," he added, when they stood in Wych Street, and he pointed to St. Clement's Danes. "I must give a minute's call in Arundel Street."

Two other men were watching them from a neighboring doorway. They took great care not to be seen.

"That's our meat, just as we were told he would be," said one to the other, indicating Frank Ellaby. "Once we secure him we'll be as well off as anyone need ever want to be. He's worth millions! You shadow him, Scooter, and make no mistake about it. If you let him give you the slip it will be as much as your skin is worth."

"You may as well come with me!"

"No thanks," laughed the first speaker. "That job's not in my way at all."

In the narrowest part of the Strand, between two churches, the detective and Frank Ellaby became separated in the roadway. Blake heard a scream, hoofs on cobblestone and squeaking metal. Blake's client was knocked down and run over by a hansom cab. He was carried to the opposite pavement in an insensible condition.

The detective feared he was dead, meaning that fate once

again laughed at him.

A tall, handsome woman pressed her way through the crowd, which at once surrounded the injured man. Her hair was chalk-white, and her eyes were coal-black. Time had treated the face tenderly. And it was determined and commanding. She was the kind of woman who could size you up in an instant, and tear you down just as quick if she pleased.

"Bring your friend to my house," she said to Blake. He thought he detected a slight accent. "It's close by—only around the corner in Norfolk Street. He may die before he can be taken to hospital. A doctor lives opposite me."

Gratefully indeed did the detective accept this opportune proposal. In addition to common altruism, strongly developed in Blake, he had selfish reasons to keep this exceedingly wealthy client alive.

It happened, fortunately, that the Norfolk Street house's front apartment was a bedroom, and here they laid the unconscious man.

In a few minutes Dr. Tuppy, from opposite, was by his side carefully examining his injuries.

"One rib fractured," he said. "Severe scalp wounds. No danger. Quiet, good nursing and my advice will soon put him on his feet again. He must not, on any account, be removed for some days. I don't know, madam—"

He paused to be supplied with the name of the lady who had called him.

"Vulpino," she said in a musical voice.

"Well, I don't know, Mrs. Vulpino, whether you can possibly allow the gentleman to stay in your rooms, but I can assure you that if you move him at present, you risk his life."

"I would not turn an injured dog from my roof," she said with a touch of emotion. "He shall stay here till he can be taken away with safety. I have an elderly woman with me who will nurse him—"

"Excellent," said the doctor.

"Believe me, he shall want for nothing."

"You are indeed a good Samaritan, madam," declared Blake. "My friend is a man of means, and any expense you may be put to—"

She closed his speech with a proud wave of her hand, which clearly indicated that she would not accept any money recompense for the inconvenience to which she was putting herself.

"Now, my dear sir," said Dr. Tuppy, "you can do nothing more for your friend. He is in excellent hands. I will see the nurse, and give her my instructions. He'll soon recover consciousness, and then he must have absolute quietness. Of course, you may come round in the morning and see how he is."

Blake, quite easy in his mind, left his new client in the house in Norfolk Street, and set about a careful consideration of the problem which had been put before him, and attending to such other matters as he had in hand.

The next day, at ten o'clock, he called to see how Ellaby was progressing.

The door was opened by a typical London lodging-house slavey.

"Well," he said, good humouredly to the girl, "how is my friend this morning?"

"Wot friend? Oh, the gent as was ill yesterday? He's gone."

"Ha. Of course he is. I guess he got up and ran after he got tired of dancing. Now, please get out of the way."

The girl didn't move. "Hello, Mr. Fancy-Pants. I told you he not here."

"Gone! Impossible! How did he go?" Suddenly a cold shiver ran down his spine and his bottom started to tingle.

"That's just what missis says when a lodger gets out without paying what he owes. Why, sir, how can I tell you how they goes?"

"Mrs. Vulpino is in, I suppose?" said the detective, as he tried to persuade himself that the girl was talking foolishly, and at random.

"She's gone too," was the answer. "That was her room he was taken into. Her time was up last night, and she went, and paid up, too. She gave me half-a-crown, and told me not to bother her when she was getting her luggage into the cab. So I didn't. I just went to sleep in the kitchen. My missis was out at the time."

"Will you let me look into Mrs. Vulpino's room?" said Blake, more perplexed than ever.

"Why, of course I will, sir," laughed the girl. "You can come and live in it if you like to pay the rent regular, and gas, and coals, and boots is hextra, and I does the boots."

There was no doubt about it. Frank Ellaby was not in the house, nor could any information be obtained as to how he had left it. To make matters worse, she knew nothing about Vulpino.

Blake went across the street to see the doctor, who simply shrugged his shoulders.

"You re all strangers to me," Tuppy said. "And I only know three things about you. First, you call me from my lunch in a dreadful hurry. Second, the removal of the patient last night was quite against my instructions, and will probably kill him. Third, I have received no fee!"

Upon hearing the word fee the detective quickly thanked the man and left. "I can't move an inch without somebody asking for money. Well, Frank Ellaby has fallen into bad hands," thought Sexton Blake, as he made his way to his office, feeling very vexed with himself. "Not only into bad hands, but I fear, powerful ones. This is bad for business. If word gets out I'll be ruined. I have to rescue him, whatever it costs me. There can be no doubt that some desperate gang followed him from Australia. They captured him the simplest way possible. I wonder if this Vulpino, foxy lady indeed, is in fact the legendary Madame Dulk. Whoever they are, they have him in their power while he's

17

quite helpless. It means a race now between my brains and another London mystery, and I'll back myself to win."

Chapter II

When Frank Ellaby regained his senses he found himself
gagged and bound hand and foot.

He was in some kind of vehicle which carried no lights.
As it jolted along a rough, dark road it rattled like a ramshackle
old four-wheeler. He was stretched inside it from the back to the
front seat. A piece of plank covered the space between, and gave
him additional support.

His injuries caused him great pain. Moving was out of
the question. At present his senses were numbed, as though the
effects of some powerful drug were still clinging to him. He
actually gave thanks that it dulled his agony. He dimly recalled

19

the accident. After that was a blank.

He consoled himself at first with the thought that he was being conveyed to some infirmary where he would find ease and receive kind treatment. But if this was the intention of those who had placed him in the cab, why was he gagged and bound?

The air grew keener, and the area through which they drove grew increasingly silent till Frank judged that they must now be in the open country. Suddenly the vehicle pulled up with a jerk which nearly sent the injured man to its other side. Stabbing pain shot through his chest.

"Wake up, my beauty," said a rough voice.

The cab door opened and Frank's body was prodded playfully with a heavy bludgeon. More pain.

"We reached our destination. You must try and walk into our picturesque country retreat, for you are a bit too heavy for me to carry."

By the aid of the bright moon Ellaby saw that the gaunt, spectral building which stood before him in murky ugliness and back from the road had been a water-mill.

The big wheel was there yet, dripping with slimy weeds. The moon's rays made the still water look green and murderous. The house itself was a forbidding structure that looked haunted.

The door of the evil place opened. A masked man carrying a lantern emerged and came towards them. His voice appeared familiar to Frank, though, at that moment, he could not identify it.

"Is it all right, Bender?" he asked, addressing the rough driver.

"Quite right. Now, my young swell, I'll just undo the strap which holds your legs, and with a little support from me, you will be able to walk inside. Why, bless me, if you haven't got a lively gold lever, as big as a turnip, and a chain strong enough to hold a horse. I'll take care of these trifles for you, and if you want any civility from me, you had better make no fuss about this little incident.

FRANK ELLABY A PRISONER.

"You see," continued the ruffian, "if you haven't any of your nonsense I can give you a touch with this"—and he tapped the prisoner's head with a life-preserver—"or you can have a dose of this."

He produced a pistol and the barrel gleamed in the moonlight.

"But there," he added with a coarse laugh, "it won't be any good for you to try on anything. We're a thousand miles from everywhere, as the saying goes, and if you try to escape all you'll find is a watery grave."

They had removed Frank's gag now. Although he was in debilitating pain he addressed them with the utmost coolness and assurance.

21

"I am too ill and weak to make any attempt to escape, especially from any place which promises warmth, rest and shelter. Pray help me in, and let me lie down"

"We have ventured to take a few liberties with you tonight," said the masked man, "but we do not contemplate hurting you, Tomorrow, however, will show us whether you're a reasonable or unreasonable man—whether we must resort to force or not."

"Tomorrow will be time enough for that or any other discussion. Tonight my pain is so great I can hardly stand. I beg you to take me indoors. The man who guards me will have an easy task."

"I am glad to see you take matters so coolly. You'll have all the attention this place affords. But let me warn you. You're as far from human aid here as though you were in your tomb."

Chapter III

"How is your patient getting on now?" the formerly masked man asked Bill Bender.

He sat before a well-spread table, enjoying a hearty meal and the latter had just returned from the room which served as Frank Ellaby's prison.

"Beautiful!" was the answer. "I never saw a man in his position take things so cool and comfortable. He couldn't be more contented in his own hotel"

"I'd rather he made a fuss. He'll prove all the more troublesome to us in the end. These calm, determined men are more difficult to deal with than excitable people. This one has

23

steel in his spine"

"We can soon knock the nonsense out of him. He's already in a lot of pain. I think he cracked a rib. What made you cover up your face with that mask tonight, Calder Dulk?"

"Obviously," he slowly drawled, "after he pays his ransom I don't want him to be able to identify me once he's free."

"Once he's free?" repeated Bender, with a low chuckle. "You don't mean that he'll ever get free? Once you got his money, he'll only be a danger to you alive. *He'll have to go where the rest have gone.*"

"I neither contemplate, nor do I recommend, violence," said Dulk, with a queer look in his eyes; "when we obtain possession of the cash I plan to leave him here, and you can do what you like with him."

"Thanks; and I shan't forget to keep my eyes on you, either," muttered the rascal.

Frank was put into a comfortable bed in a warm room, and he was well-fed, although he didn't have much of an appetite. The good news was that whoever bandaged his injuries had done the work with some skill.

There was no window to the apartment and escape was prevented by an iron-bound oaken door secured by bolts and a heavy metal bar on the outside.

Except for the fact that he was a prisoner in that sinister building, and probably in imminent peril of his life, he might have felt as contented there as in any other place.

After a long and grave consideration of his present position he came to the unjust conclusion that Sexton Blake was behind his kidnapping.

"Yes," thought Frank, 'it must be Blake. Not another soul in London knows who I am, or what I'm worth! I wonder how much he'll want to set me free? I wonder whether I'll give in to his cursed demands! I don't think so. He's playing a dangerous game, and he'll suffer for it, unless they kill me outright. I don't remember the accident, but my helplessness may have suggested to him a cunning plot. Opportunity is the great tempter. I suppose tomorrow my gaolers will tell me their intentions."

When he awoke the following day he felt refreshed and so hungry that he looked forward eagerly for the appearance of breakfast. He considered his returning appetite a good sign. His rib still hurt, however, and the drugs had worn off.

But Frank had a remarkably strong constitution, which travel, hardship and exposure had hardened, and not shattered. So in spite of Dr. Tuppy's prognostications, his sudden and queer removal had not retarded his recovery. He felt that a few days would see him on his feet again, and in fair health.

His only visitor the next day was Bill Bender. He brought a jug of coffee and a couple of slices of bread and butter.

"We are not going to fill you up with high-class food," said the man, "because it might fire your blood, and we mean to keep you nice and cool."

Frank still welcomed this fare, rough as it was. "This coffee is surprisingly good," he said.

"It's my little secret," said Bender, "I add a pinch of salt.

"Now," continued the ruffian, drawing a packet of papers from his pocket, "I'm going to leave these things with you for your careful and best consideration. One is a cheque on the London Joint Stock Bank. Don't look at me like that! We've got friends in Paris who told us which was your London bank."

"Gervaise, of course," Frank thought; "he planned this with Sexton Blake. I have plunged my head right into the hornet's nest."

"All you have to do," continued Bender with a grin, "is to sign this cheque, and then, in case you should not have so much cash at that bank as we want, here's a little power of attorney for you to put your name to. It authorizes Mr. Cornelius Brown to realize on any stocks or shares, bonds or certificates, personal or real estate, you may possess. Once you have signed these different documents, and we have taken our cut, you'll be free to leave this place and enjoy yourself as you may think best. So it just rests with you, Mr. Frank Ellaby, how long you remain here. We can wait for years, if necessary. *You have not one living person on earth likely to trouble themselves whether you are alive or dead!*"

How true this was Frank knew only too well, and to his sorrow.

26

"Who is Cornelius Brown?"

"Does it matter?"

"I can't prevent you from leaving the papers here," he said quietly; "but I will never sign one of them as long as I live!"

"That's what you think now, old son, but we'll make you change your mind soon enough."

"I should be a fool to sign." Frank spoke carelessly. "So long as you want my authorization to those papers, you'll keep me alive; but once that's done, you'll have to kill me. I've seen your face."

"Well, how clever you are! But, look here; this matter has been put into my hands, and I'm going to work it off quick. I don't suppose you are a bit more frightened of death than I am; but there's something worse than that, *and it's torture*. If you won't come to any reasonable terms, *I'll starve you into submission!* Do you hear?"

"You cur!" said Frank, contemptuously. "Why, you would run a mile from me, if I had my strength, and we were on equal terms. As it is, I'll bring you to the earth!"

On a little bedside table the man had placed a metal inkpot and a pen, with the papers he wished Frank to sign. He seized this pewter inkstand and hurled it with all the force he could command, full in the face of his brutal custodian.

The blow was unexpected, and Bill dropped to the ground like a log.

Frank thought that the moment of his escape had come,

and he tried to struggle into his clothes.

Unfortunately he was so weak that he had to sink back onto the bed, and cling to it, trembling from the effects of his recent exertions.

"I didn't think this through," he said to himself. "Damn my temper." There were tears in his eyes.

This gave Bender time to regain his feet, and he soon had his prisoner back between the sheets and replaced the inkwell.

"So that's a sample of temper, is it?" snarled Bill. "I'll look out for you in the future. You take my advice. Sign those papers while you have a chance. I'm a bit of a rough guy to deal with when I'm put out, and you have marked my forehead for life. Until those papers are signed you don't get bite nor sup from me."

"You already told me you're going to starve me!"

With a curse Bill left Frank Ellaby to recover from his prostration as best he could.

For two days Frank had neither food nor drink given him.

In one way he suffered terribly, but his natural stubbornness and positive attitude helped his injuries to heal up in a miraculously short space of time, despite his growing dehydration.

He then began to consider whether, after all, he had not better attach his signature to the documents which were still at the side of his bed. If he did not do the wretches' bidding it was certain they would starve him to death.

He decided he could lose nothing by agreeing to their terms. If he ever got free he promised himself that he would punish severely Gervaise and Blake. He hoped, too, that he would be able to make them disgorge the money they had wrenched from him.

The next time Bender put his head into the room, with the question whether his prisoner had come to his senses yet, Ellaby said:

"I signed everything. Bring me something to eat and drink. When you have your money you let me go."

"Unlikely," said Bill, with a coarse laugh, as he thrust the papers into his heavy overcoat's breast pocket. "Now, listen to me. If you hadn't been so obstinate I would have done fair and honest by you. But you've been pig-headed, and you've kept me from my pleasures. More than that, you marked my face. The consequence of which is that *I'm going to leave you here to starve. You can't escape. No one come will come to you. Here you'll stay and slowly die.*"

"Liar!" Frank yelled. "You never intended to let me go. You're just using that as an excuse."

If Bender heard him he gave no indication and left the room, bolting and barring the door behind him.

"He tells the truth about one thing," groaned Frank, "I'm finished. I'll be dead from dehydration in a day or two."

Chapter IV

"So far all my searching has been in vain. I have failed to find any trace of Frank Ellaby."

So said Sexton Blake to his colleague Jules Gervaise to whom he had telegraphed directly after the millionaire disappeared.

"I blame myself very much for thees catastrophe," said the French Gervaise, gloomily. "I deedn't tell you everything. I should have deescribed that woman to you, and have put you on your guard against her. She was as anxious to secure Ellaby as he was to find and punish her. I also deeedn't tell you that she approach me first, and wanted me to shadow him. After

30

eenvestigating her and deescovering that she was a criminal I approach him and he hire me to gather information concerning her. She must have found out because she suddenly left Paris. I eentended coming to England, to put you on her track, and I feegure that you quick discovery of her would bring a substantial reward. You have already guessed that Madame Vulpino and Mrs. Calder Dulk are one person. Thees unfortunate affair has played havoc with my plans. Mr. Ellaby's enemies have the, how you say, top hand."

"Upper hand. Are you saying it was not an accident?"

"Who knows? She may have planned eet, she may have acted on opportunity. Even the near-by lodging was just to be by your office, where she expected heem to be."

"I've since learned that on the night of his disappearance," said Blake, "the woman, accompanied by a shabbily-dressed man drove from Norfolk Street to Charing Cross Station, where she took two tickets for Paris. She and her companion both entered the Continental train, but it is quite certain they never went by it. They must have left it when it was on the point of starting."

"The booking to France was a mere blind—to lead you on a false scent. There can be no doubt that the woman ees steell een London, and probably not far off. Very likely the man who accompany her was Dulk. Witheen a day or so I expect someone weell come to the London Joint Stock Bank with a cheque signed by the meessing man. As we have warned the authorities

31

at the bank to detain any such person, I hope to reach the conspirators that way. There can be no doubt that their object ees to extort money from their prisoner."

"Assuming it's that easy, and that they are so foolish. If not, there may be another way," said Blake.

"*Qu'est-ce que c'est?*"

"The 'Red Lights,' my friend."

"I repeat, what's that?"

"It's a new and formidable society of professional lawbreakers of every class. The idea springs from the fertile brain of a young, well-educated fellow named Leon Polti. It was his idea to join together into one powerful association the most expert operators in all branches of crime. The cleverest burglar throws in his lot with the most accomplished forger, and so on through the whole list of police offences. The notion is a brotherhood, organized crime, if you will, with meeting places and correspondents all over the country, working for their own common good, and against honest people. If Polti could realize his highest ideal and conduct such a gigantic organization, on strictly business principles, and with keen method, I fear the police would be beaten at every turn. Luckily, rogues never do agree on anything for long.

"They observe no laws—not even their own. So Politi's vast scheme will remain a dream, and nothing else, to the end of time. This case looks something like the work of his gang. Watching and waiting for the rich man coming from Australia,

32

and sending the woman over to Paris to shadow him suggests his methods. I daresay I can find him. We'll see if we can discover anything of his doings."

At this point their conversation was interrupted by the appearance of a shaggy, flaming head of red hair, which thrust itself into the office through the half-opened doorway.

"Well," interrogated Blake, "what do you want?"

"Please, gov'nor, I'm the boy wot stands about the top of Essex Street, selling papers, and you've given me many a brown, you has."

A body followed the head, and there stood disclosed to the two detectives a short, bright-faced boy who resembled an animated bundle of rages. His tattered trousers barely touched his knees and strips of time-eaten cloth fluttered round his thin, discoloured arm.

"I've got no browns for you today," said Blake, waving his hand impatiently.

"Oh yes, you has sir," the street boy answered with a knowing shake of his glowing locks. "Wait till you 'ear wot I've to tell yer, and then I think you'll be good for a bob' It's like this 'ere. Tommy Roundhead says as 'ow you want to find out about a 'toff' as was taken out of a house in Arundel Street, late Thursday night. Well, I can tell you all about that 'ere. 'Cos, why? I helped in the job myself."

"If you can help me to find that gentleman," said Blake, with sudden energy, "I'll make a man of you! We won't trouble about shillings. Pounds and pounds shall be spent on you."

"We can decide what to do when we have heard his tale," said Gervaise, nervously, as he too was down on his luck.

"It's like this, gov'nor. I was walking down Arundel Street, wondering where I should pitch myself for the night, when a four-wheeler drives up, and stops at that house. The driver jumps off the box, and I sees, at once, that he weren't a reg'lar cabby. 'Ere young Vesuvius!' 'ee cries, ''old the 'osses 'ed.' The door of the 'ouse opens without him knocking or ringing. I sees that there's a sort of bed made up in the cab. In a minute or two the driver comes out with another man. Between them they carries a third man, who, if he ain't dead, 'as lost 'is senses. They puts this helpless chap inside, and the coachman springs on to his box again. 'I shall be there before you,' said the man standing on the pavement. He puts his 'and in 'is pocket, and after fumbling about a bit, he pull out 'arf a sovereign. 'Take that,' he says to me, 'I ain't got noffink smaller.' He walks away quick.

"'Well,' finks I, 'if I gets 'arf a quid for 'olding the 'oss while they puts the swell into the cab, perhaps I shall get a bit more if I'm there to 'old it when they takes 'im *hout*.' So I gets up on the back of the cab, and clings on. But, bless you! I was taken right away to Barking. I didn't get off because I wasn't sure the cab would be coming back again. At last we stops before a tumble-down old water-mill. Then the driver brings out a blunderbuss or somfink deadly, and a reg'lar hold-fashioned

34

life preserver. I take to me 'eels in case they should want to give me one on the 'ed. I waits about hoping to see the cab go back. But they puts it in the stable there, and I 'as to walk. I fall in with a tramp, and he sneaks my half-sovereign. Then the police collars me for being a wagabond, and that's how it is I ain't been at my hold pitch the last day or two."

"This is news indeed," exclaimed Gervaise. "Can you lead us to this old mill?"

"It's a hawful lonely place," said the boy, "but I fink I can find it again."

"*Allons-y,*" suggested Gervaise. "*Immediatemente.*"

"Right. We must lose no time," agreed Blake, meditatively, "but we need to go to work with extreme caution. I don't like that remote water-mill. It sounds murderous my ears. If our man is

SEXTON BLAKE, DETECTIVE.

still there and alive his gaolers may get desperate. The quickest way will be to take the train to Barking."

"Can't do it, gov'nor," declared the lad; "I'll never find the place if I don't go the same way as that four-wheeler did."

They hired a hansom and it took half a day to light on the spot where Bender had threatened Frank Ellaby with bludgeon and pistol.

35

"The place is deserted," said Blake. "I fear the worst."

"We shall have no deeffïculty getting een," said Gervaise, as he threw the weight of his body against a rotten and ill-secured back door, which at once flew open.

The rats infesting the place scampered before them as they walked through the musty passages and gloomy rooms.

Upstairs they came on a heavy door, barred and bolted on the outside.

Their hearts beat high as they undid these fastenings. They felt sure there were on the point of entering the room where Ellaby had been kept prisoner.

Neither spoke as they entered. Blake did not expect to find him alive, since he didn't answer their shouts when they entering the building.

"Empty," said Gervaise. "What a strong room eet ees. Eet might have been built for a prison cell. He has been here, that's quite clear. There ees his bed, hees writing materials—"

"And" said Blake, "an absence of water and of other food."

"They leave heem to starve to death!" Gervaise added excitedly, "but he has escaped by tearing the fire-grate from its settings."

Indeed the grate lay on the floor, and the back of the fireplace revealed a gaping hole.

"See how loose the bricks are behind eet. He could not have had great deeffïculty een making the hole through which he must have crawled. There is a room beyond—long, narrow. *Bon!* We must follow hees example, and see where it leads."

"His footprints on the dusty floor are still here," said Blake. "The open window at the end shows he escaped that way. Why has he not communicated with me?"

"Because," answered Gervaise impressively, "hees body lies at the bottom of that steeell, black-looking pool. You observe, this window ees exactly over the old wheel of the water-mill. He must have stepped on to eet. His weight would make eet revolve; he would be hurled eento the water. Probably one of the flanges strike hees head, and make him eensensible. Then the weeds catch him een their embrace.

"See! There ees hees hat floating on the green scum! We must have thees water dragged!"

As soon as they could procure drags and other aids, the pond was thoroughly searched.

After some hour's work and with much difficulty, they brought a corpse to the bank, about which lank weeds still clung.

"Unhappily, we are too late to preserve the life of Frank Ellaby. The one thing left for us ees to make our very best effort to bring hees murderers to justice," said Gervaise.

"I jest wants to be paid," said the newsboy who brought them there.

Chapter V

In the old-fashioned Sussex village of Downslow, in an
ivy-clad rectory's library sat Rev. Frederick Briarton. He was
engaged in grave conversation with Ernest Truelove, a farmer's
son who was on the eve of leaving his old home for London. The
lad intended to enter medical school and hoped to become a
surgeon.

"I won't lie to you about how happy I am that Rose loves
you," said the clergyman. "I believe in you, and in your high
regard for truth and honour. I'm an old man, and it's idle for me
to hope that I'll be here be much longer. But I'll pass peacefully
knowing that Rose has will be with someone who'll look after

38

her and protect her"

"I wish you wouldn't talk like that," said the lad.

"Fuh. But, listen, my dear boy, I have a secret to tell you, something you should know before you commit to this engagement."

"Nothing can possibly make me change my mind," said Ernest fervently.

"Prepare yourself for a shock, my friend. *Rose is not my daughter!* I do not even know who her parents are."

"You have succeeded in surprising me," said the young man. "But I love Rose for herself; I don't care who she is!"

"Indeed, I knew you would feel that way. Listen. Many years ago I was chaplain to one of Her Majesty's prisons. A few days before I resigned that appointment to commence duties at a small living in Yorkshire one of the female convicts, a handsome and accomplished woman, sent for me, and upon her knees implored me to protect a little girl her arrest and sentence had compelled her to leave in the care of some rough, illiterate people living at Hammersmith. She said that the child was not her own, that it had a great future before it, and that when she was released she would repay me for my trouble, and restore the child to its proper sphere. As I had not been blessed with any children of my own I was ready enough to adopt Rose. My poor wife grew attached to her, and she was brought up as our own daughter. The time soon came when I began to feel terror lest her convict guardian should appear at our home, and claim our darling daughter.

"Not long after my wife passed, by the will of an uncle I was practically compelled to change my old name of Sparrow to the one I now bear—Briarton. I have moved about a good deal, too, and perhaps that is why the woman has not found me. I am glad to have eluded her. It would go very much against my moral train to have to deliver up so sweet and simple a girl to a woman who has once worn a convict's dress. I have never had the courage to tell Rose the truth. She firmly believes herself to be my child."

"I wish you hadn't told me," said the young man. "I don't see any good come from telling her, but now I feel like I'm lying to her. It would be cruel to tell her the truth now, and no useful purpose would be served. She's too good for me to believe that her parents were bad. I'll work hard, and in a little over three years will secure my diploma; then I can give her a name which shall be her very own. Well, mine, but you know what I mean; and then she can defy anyone who may wish to claim her."

After this Ernest spent a long time with the young lady, until he had to drive to the station and catch his train. They had repeated their mutual vows over and over.

When evening prayers were said in the vicarage the rector introduced a fervent one for the safety and prosperity of Ernest Truelove, amid the pitfalls and temptations of the huge metropolis.

40

Meanwhile this young gentleman, having spent an hour in Brighton, was dashing on to London at express speed, his regrets at leaving his old friends and the scenes of his youth lightened by thoughts of his upcoming adventures.

Sexton Blake was not wrong about his understanding of luck and chance, since fate was about to intervene in his behalf most egregiously. Truelove's only fellow-passenger was a young gent who looked about his own age, but he might have been older. Slight in build, with creamy skin and large, dark, fascinating eyes, a round smooth chin, and a delicate mouth, he was pretty and effeminate in appearance. And yet there lurked in his very graceful movement a suspicion of sinewy and uncommon strength.

The two had easily fallen into conversation, and this had led to an exchange of cards.

The stranger's bore the name Leon Polti. The man honestly enjoyed Ernest's company and immediately took a liking to him.

"So," said Leon, to whom the innocent Ernest had confided much of his past history and many of his plans for the future, "you want comfortable lodgings in the centre of London? Ah! Now I don't think you can do better than take up your quarters at the house where my sister and I are temporarily located—99, Bernard Street, Russell Square. It's no distance from Charing Cross Hospital. The landlady is the most obliging creature I ever met, and the cooking is capital. I know she has a

41

bed and sitting-room to let. Probably you don't mind if they are a bit high up. You can drive home with me tonight. There'll be no harm in seeing the place, even if you should elect not to take the apartments."

"I am very much obliged to you," said Ernest. "I have no doubt the place will suit me very well indeed. I suppose, though, I shall have to go to a hotel tonight?"

"Not a bit of it! If you like the accommodation, Mrs. Dulk, the landlady, will make you perfectly comfortable at once."

After arriving and seeing the accommodations Ernest was charmed with the house and with his new friends.

The same evening he dined with Polti, and he saw that this gentleman lived in quite high style. The table was spread with delicacies, in and out of season, and there were famous wines.

"My sister is out of town tonight," said his host. "I hope to introduce you to her tomorrow."

On the following morning he encountered a dark young lady on the stairs. The likeness to Leon Polti was so striking that he could not doubt her identity, so he ventured to address her.

"Oh, yes," she said, with a laugh, which exposed a set of brilliant teeth, "I'm Nizza Polti. My brother has told me so much about you. I hope we shall be great friends. Some business has called him away; he will not be back for a few days. But," she added, "Mrs. Dulk generally sits with me in the evening, and any time you like we shall be glad if you will join us."

The days passed very pleasantly with Ernest. Some evenings he saw Nizza, and on others Leon. Their own affairs so fell out that they were never able to be together when young Truelove was in the house.

One evening as Leon was sitting with the medical student in the latter's room Mrs. Dulk tapped at the door, and brought word that a gentleman waited below to see Polti on urgent business.

"Bother him!" said Leon. "Can't he come in the morning?"

"No. he says it is imperative that you see him now."

"He shall wait till I have finished this cigar, at any rate. Tell him so, whoever he may be. I hate these inquisitive people," he added with a yawn to Ernest.

When he did at last deign to descend the stairs he found Calder Dulk waiting for him. He took him into another room.

"You have an odd way of disturbing one at most inconvenient moments," said Leon. "Well, what is it you want me for?"

"The rat in his cage has eaten his cheese," replied Dulk, harshly, annoyed at the other's assumption of cool indifference. Polti just stared at him. "In other words, Mr. Frank Ellaby has signed all the papers you made out for him to put his signature to. I've got them on me. It's for you to turn them into gold. Our part of the business is finished, and that has been the roughest

43

and the worst section of it. Now you can put in some of your 'fine' work, as you call it."

"I'm afraid you have come in a sneering mood, Dulk," Polti drawled his words out lazily. "And really it does not become so jovial a fellow as yourself. *What has been done with Ellaby?*"

"I left him to Bender. *You* know what he generally does with them."

"It's always force, and never persuasion, with you people," said Leon contemptuously.

"Don't blame me for what he does. You know how he is. These papers seem to be all right," he continued. "They'll have my attention as soon as possible, and you will all know the result"

"That won't do for me," said Dulk fiercely. "I mean having the lion's share of this plunder. Why, if it hadn't been for me you wouldn't have known Frank Ellaby's existence. But for my wife's promptitude it might have taken you months to capture him. Those papers represent an actual little gold mine. It is through our work, and through the work of no one else, that they have been obtained, and we mean being paid in full! You talk about us all being equal. You're like the man in the play. He wanted his followers to be equal so long as he was chief. No doubt you would like to be crowned 'Monarch of Criminals,' and 'King of Crime,' and all that kind of thing; but we are not quite such fools as to give way to you."

"You amuse me, Dulk," said Leon, throwing himself back in his chair, and smiling dangerously. "Perhaps you will condescend to remember that, but for me, there would have been no house in Arundel Street to take your victim to—the man you have twice plundered. But for me there would have been no old mill in which to torture him into subjection. But for me you would not now have good broadcloth on your back. But for me the only possible roof for you would be the strong one of the gaol. You want the lion's share of the money? You shall have it all, my friend. Take back your papers; do what you will with them. I wash my hands of the affair, of you, of your wife. You cannot play either the role of knave or honest man. Well, I am better without you. Good night."

He turned to leave and his visitor panicked. "Leon, Leon," pleaded Dulk, with a white, anxious face, "don't talk like that! You know I don't dare work those papers! Come, come; forgive me! I spoke hastily; I didn't mean what I said. Take the papers again. Work as you choose with them; I have no conditions."

"Conditions!" repeated Leon. "The world must turn inside out before *you* will ever be able to dictate to *me*. Leave those documents. Go away. I will see what can be done. It's a risky business, and I know the hazard better than any of you. If a hitch occurs, there must be instant flight from here."

"Yes," said Polti to himself when he was alone; "I see that I am in the most danger from my own followers. They would kill me to gain possession of Ellaby's money. Dulk is the most likely man to strike the first blow. Knowing where the danger is I can avoid it. Extreme caution and swift flight will save me, and nothing else. I thank thee, Fate, for throwing that innocent young Ernest Truelove in my way. I do like him, but business is business."

On the following morning the student again met Nizza Polti on the stirs.

"My brother has been unexpectedly called away again this morning before you were awake," she said in her pretty way, shedding the full light of her eyes on his face. "He wants you to do a small favour for him, and I am sure you will. It's only to get a cheque cashed at the London Joint Stock Bank, and meet him tonight at Charing Cross Railway Station with the money. He's going on to Paris with it."

"I shall be delighted to be of any service to him, and to you," said Ernest, bowing. "Why! this cheque is for £20,000! Quite a fabulous amount!"

"My brother's transactions often run into five figures," she answered, with a smile. "If the cheque were for a small sun, I could do the business myself. He prefers to trust it to you, because you are stronger and cleverer than I am. Banks distrust dealing with women."

"Directly after my breakfast I will go to the bank," declared Ernest, in his impulsive way.

"There is not such a great hurry. So long as you are at

46

the bank by eleven o'clock, that will do."

If luck were indeed a virus as Blake mused, than the house of Mrs. Dulk had the fever. For a second time it's inhabitants were to defy any reasonable chance. Just as Ernest was leaving the house a cab drew up at the door. To his great surprise, it contained Rose and the Rev. Frederick Briarton.

Mrs. Dulk, always watching and listening, was standing at the dining room window and she had a clear view of them.

She drew back hastily. She was literally shaking all over. She contained herself, as she wanted to dance.

"I cannot believe this!" she said to herself. "The clergyman to whom I confided the child. He comes right to my door! How can this be? What are the odds? One person in twenty million! The needle has not only removed itself from the haystack, it delivers itself to my door. Am I dreaming? It's quite impossible, But I don't doubt my own eyes. I recognize Rose, grown into a beautiful woman. I will lose no time in regaining my prize. My husband and Polti and the rest may have their big hauls, but I shall now be better off than any of them. It's almost enough for me to believe in God."

Inside the sitting room her lodger greeted his guests. "Dad had me come up to London by the very first train on some business in the city." Rose explained. She was flushed with excitement, and with the delight she felt at seeing her lover again. "So I coaxed him to let me come, too."

"We thought we would give you a surprise," laughed the

47

vicar," "and join you in a little lunch, if you have such a handy thing in the house."

"Only too delighted to see you," said Ernest; "but I must go downtown myself. We can all go together and talk as we go.

"My business is with the Joint Stock Bank," he added, "and it won't take long. After that I shall be entirely at your service. What do you think, Mr. Briarton? I'm going to change a cheque for twenty thousand pounds!"

The figures were sufficiently large to impress the rural clergyman, and to awe Rose.

Ernest briefly explained how he chanced to be in possession of so valuable a piece of paper.

After arriving they watched as he, with a great air of importance (which he could not resist), entered the bank. They saw him emerge from its portals, and then a dreadful thing happened.

A tall, broad man tapped him on the shoulder.

Before he could say a word a pair of handcuffs were thrust on his wrists. Two other men came from across the road with a seeming air of authority. They were seized also, and treated the same way.

The police had taken Ernest Truelove into custody. They had also arrested Mssrs. Gervaise and Blake, very much to the complete dismay of both detectives.

Calder Dulk and Leon Polti watched these proceedings from a safe corner, and then made off with all speed possible.

Poor Rose uttered a cry of distress and the Reverend Mr. Briarton sprang onto the pavement and was at once in the midst of the excited group, standing shoulder-to-shoulder with Frank Ellaby.

Chapter VI

"So I made a good haul and caught you all at once," said
Ellaby, with a grim smile. "I'm sorry you have turned out a
rogue, Gervaise, because I trusted you. I did hope that you,
Sexton Blake, were honest; yet you have joined in with this frog
to conspire against me. As for you," he added, addressing Ernest
Truelove and putting his finger inches from his nose, "you have
a noble, manly face, which makes me sorry to see you associated
with this scum."

"I don't know what all this means," declared Briarton,
"but I do aver that this young gentleman never did a
dishonourable action in his life, and if you dare to detain him, it

will be at your own peril. He was simply asked to get this cheque cashed by people who lodge in the house where he has apartments."

"It was Leon Polti's sister," Truelove commenced.

"I knew it!" Blake interrupted, He and Gervaise had been watching the bank hoping to spot Polti or Dulk. "This, as I suspected, is indeed the work of the Red Lights, and I hope we'll be able to capture and convict the whole gang. I forgive you, Mr. Ellaby, for thinking I had something to do with your kidnapping; but had you gone to Scotland Yard instead of to the City Police you would have heard that Gervaise and myself have toiled day and night to rescue you. Only yesterday we discovered the old mill. We had the pond dragged, and we found a body, which, at first, we thought was yours..."

"No, I am still alive," said Frank, "though I did get a ducking there. I hope, Blake, your tale is true. Is there no communication between the Yard and the police precincts?"

"If we all drive to the metropolitan police headquarters you will soon be satisfied on that point. It's my opinion, Mr. Ellaby, that this young man has simply been the dupe for the daring Polti crowd."

"I am a clergyman of the Church of England," said Briarton; "and I have known Ernest Truelove for many years. I am convinced he is incapable of committing a criminal action. I must insist on his immediate release from custody."

"Oh, Rose, Rose!" said Ernest, as his *fiancée* joined the

throng. "I do wish you have been spared the pain of seeing me so disgraced."

"So your name is Rose?" questioned Frank Ellaby, as the name brought a rush of memories to him. "Many years ago I had a little girl stolen from me bearing that name. She must be about

"THE PRISONER HURLED THE PEWTER INKSTAND, WITH ALL THE FORCE HE COULD COMMAND, FULL IN THE FACE OF HIS CUSTODIAN."

your age now. I would give much to find her."

"That is a matter we can discuss some other time," declared the rector, and with such significance that a sudden hope sprung up in Frank's heart. "Ernest Truelove must be released!"

The police officers in charge agreed to ferry the lot to Scotland Yard. It took very little time to disprove the charges against Messrs. Blake and Gervaise, to whom Ellaby made a most handsome apology.

Likewise he was persuaded to withdraw every imputation against Ernest Truelove; and later, when he knew more of him, he decided to make him reparation for the wrong to which he had been subjected.

They all journeyed to Bernard Street, hoping to effect the capture of Mrs. Dulk and Nizza Polti, if not of Leon himself.

No one answered their repeated knocks or continuous bell ringing. Gervais kicked in the door. The house was empty.

"The birds have flown," said Blake. "No doubt Mr. Truelove was shadowed to the bank. Really, I expected better from Polti. When Ernest was seen to be taken into custody the warning note was sounded, and the ducks have taken unto themselves wings. Gervaise and I will see that the railway stations and the wharves are watched. Every effort shall be made to prevent the culprits' escape. Now that we know them there shouldn't be any difficulty about it. You gentlemen had best make yourselves comfortable at some good family hotel where I can visit you later on and report my progress. Say the Silver Bell at Charing Cross. I really don't think you can help us now in any way. Too many cooks, you know."

"All my personal belongs are here," said Ernest, ruefully looking up the stairs.

"I daresay you will get your luggage all right," returned Gervaise, with a smile, "you'll have to come back for them with

53

a police escort. We have not a moment to lose. You need to ensconce yourselves in a hotel and out of sight. "

Even as he spoke, Calder Dulk and Nizza Polti stood on the platform of King's Cross Station ready to step into a fast train soon to start for one of the Northern centres.

The appearance of Frank Ellaby outside the bank had filled Dulk with the direst consternation. He judged that England was no longer safe, especially as Ernest was in custody, and could put them on the track of Madame Dulk, who had gone he knew not where.

"Ah!" he said, when he and Nizza had settled themselves in the carriage, and the train was almost on the move, "we shall get out of London all right, and then entire escape won't be so very difficult."

The whistle sounded, and the great engine gave one mighty gasp of relief.

There were on the move, when the door was torn open, and a man threw himself into the carriage.

"Keep still," Bill Bender yelled, placing himself opposite them. "If you move an inch I'll shoot you both like the dogs you are."

He pointed a pistol at each head.

"How did you find us?" said Dulk.

"Wasn't hard. I followed you from the house. So," he continued, "you've got my share—me, who did all the work, too! It isn't the first time you tried that game, but it'll be the last."

"All the work," said Dulk. "It must have been pretty hard to not feed a prisoner."

"Shut up," Bender said. "You look very pretty in that woman's disguise, Leon; but it won't work with me. I always swore if a pal played me false that I would kill him. And now here you are."

They knew that their first stop was Peterborough, and that they were completely at the mercy of this desperate man.

Chapter VII

It was some time before the two men recovered from
their surprise.

"Don't be a fool, Bill. We've not got a farthing of Frank
Ellaby's money. The game is up; the detectives are after the lot
of us. We are flying out of London, and mean to lie quiet in the
country for a time; that's why we're on this train."

It was Calder Dulk who spoke, half pleadingly, and with
somewhat of a reassuring tone to Bender, who still covered him
and Leon/Nizza Polti with his pistols. Dulk looked helpless.

"You always were an idiot, Bender," said Polti, coolly,
talking in his natural voice.

56

The disguise was so perfect that only very few of his own followers knew that he did not possess a sister. By the aid of this change of costume he had more than once deceived his confederates, and passed freely out from among them.

"Put those silly things down. They are more likely to hurt you than me. I'm actually glad you turned up," Leon added in a business-like manner. "I wanted to see you. I fancy we may yet get hold of that money, and want your help, my friend Bender."

They had emerged from the King's Cross tunnel and were beginning to whiz along at a rate which soon promised exciting speed.

"None of that for me," said Bill. "I've had enough of you. Now then, young gentleman in the skirts, tumble up the gold. You had the cheque right enough, and you've got the money."

"Certainly I had the cheque," acknowledged Leon quietly, "but you don't suppose I was going to be so foolish as to present it myself? There was always a 33 percent chance pf getting caught. I hoped that we could have gotten the money before the police warned the bank, but, alas, no. And it's your fault."

"No," growled Bill, "instead you've been clever enough to leave me to be the only one who can be identified as being connected with this job. One wears a mask and the other hides himself. Then you try to do me out of the money and leave me to swing, while you enjoy yourselves with wine and women, if that's what Leon likes."

"I'm also at risk. I sent a young country friend of mine to the bank to get Ellaby's cheque cashed," Leon spoke impressively. "So I can be identified just like you. He knows my face, just as Ellaby saw yours. I suppose he got the money. Dulk and I watched him from a safe distance to see if things were all right. All we know is that when our young friend came out he was immediately arrested. But just pay particular attention to this, Bill—*Frank Ellaby was there, too, waiting for him!*"

"What!" exclaimed Bill, so astonished at the news that he relaxed a trifle of his vigilance.

"That's why we don't have the money, stupid."

"You lie!! How could he have escaped from the mill? I was sure he would be a corpse by now. He won't rest till he finds me. Yah!" he exclaimed, with a sudden change of demeanor, "you think I'm a kid, and you're trying to put me off with these fairy tales till we stop somewhere, where you think you can get help. Come on, pay up, or I'll fire."

"I saw him too," said Dulk.

"It's true," said Polti. "When we stop you can wire London and verify it yourself. Don't be so thick-headed, Bill; I tell you we have not got the money. Besides, I should never think of swindling *you*; you're far too useful to us. Why don't you search us? Perhaps that will satisfy you. You can start with me."

"So I will," said the thoughtless ruffian, laying his pistols by his side.

Leon was full of tricks. He was unsure whether after searching them and finding nothing if Bender would let them go. This proposal was only a ruse to put him off his guard, and to take his weapons.

It would have succeeded admirably had not Leon been impatient. He stretched his white hand over to secure the weapons before Bill had half risen from his seat.

The burly bully saw what was intended, and Leon was felled to the floor of the carriage, rendered insensible, and his body kicked under a seat in less time than it took Bender to stand up.

Thinking *his* opportunity had come, Dulk now sprung on the tough, only to be received by his powerful grip. A mighty struggle was about to ensue, since Dulk was a man of weight and muscle.

Nothing ever now would persuade Bender that they told him the truth. His teeth were set. His eyes stood out of his head. His whole system throbbed with one idea, and it was fierce—to crush Dulk.

This thought so absorbed his every faculty that he did not hear the rush through the air of the train, the rattle of the carriages or the frequent wild shrieks of the engine.

No pleadings for mercy from human tongue could stop him.

Dulk's veins rose upon his forehead, knotted and black. His face was horror-stricken when he realized the extent of Bender's fury. He knew that a relentless demon was grappling with him, and he could escape only by superhuman effort.

Strive his utmost he did, straining every muscle and nerve.

At one moment the two stood silent, and looking as firm as a pair of Roman wrestlers cut in marble. When the train gave a lurch they were thrown heavily with it. Then came a fierce , panting struggle on the floor. Some seconds one had the advantage, to be quickly wrenched from him by the other.

As they managed at last to struggle to their feet, they never for an instant released their holds.

A thick hot breath fanned their cheeks as a blast from a furnace. The compartment's solid seating on each side of them created a narrow passage making it difficult for either to throw the other. So each strove with slow, persistent effort to reach the other's pulsating throat.

Bill Bender was eventually won this deadly effort.

As his thumb and finger closed on Dulk's neck, a groan of triumph escaped him. Now he could throw his whole weight against his victim, for with the latter's lack of breath the muscles of his arms and legs relaxed.

The two fell against the carriage door. A third of Dulk's body was already out of the open window, which had no protecting rail in its center.

Just then they were entering a tunnel.

"You're done!" growled Bill, lifting up the man's legs and letting him drop out into the darkness.

A crimson flash of light from the fire of the engine illuminated his ghastly white face as he was swallowed up by the relentless black outside the train.

"It's Leon Polti who has the money; that's certain, or he would not be got up like a girl," muttered Bill, and he at once com-menced to roughly search that gentleman.

"The other has got it after all!" he cried, in disgust. "All that money's on the line for any navvy or

"A THIRD OF DULK'S BODY WAS ALREADY OUT OF THE OPEN
WINDOW. . . JUST THEN THEY WERE ENTERING A TUNNEL."

porter to find. I got to have a try for it."

The signal towards the exit of the tunnel was against the train, and it slowed. Bill took advantage of this opportunity and he dropped gently off the footboard into the gloom.

Leon, now alone, sprang to his feet, and taking down a small bag from the luggage-rail he quickly made a complete transformation in his dress. "He really isn't very bright, is he? He didn't even look at the luggage. Not that it would have helped him. Oh, well."

When the train stopped at Peterborough he stepped gingerly from his carriage and appeared in dress that would have befitted the most exacting up-to-date Bond Street swell.

"I'm glad Bill and Dulk are gone," he reflected, with an amiable smile. "They were beginning to get troublesome."

Chapter VIII

While the detectives pursued their investigations, Frank
Ellaby's party engaged quarters at the cozy and eminently
respectable hostelry the Silver Bell. Truelove made arrangements
to get his luggage. He and Rose went off to a corner by
themselves. Briarton and Ellaby exchanged confidences.

"From what you have told me," said the latter, "I have
little doubt, in my own mind, that your Rose and the little girl
my dying sister entrusted to my care are one and the same. How
this could be I cannot fathom. She's one girl out of millions of
people. Nobody is this lucky."

"The Lord works in mysterious ways," said the vicar.

"The woman from whom you received her said no idle words when she declared that the child had a great future before her, for I can give her much wealth.

"Though I never liked Calder Dulk's wife, I did not regard her as a criminal until she robbed me, so the news isn't surprising. I had no idea she was still looking for me.

"Someone once said that we all live our lives twice over. Certainly, our experiences have a way of repeating themselves in the strangest manner.

"I quite agree with you, that it would be unwise to say anything to the young lady at present touching her real identity. But I fear we shall never discover it, unless we can force that woman Dulk to give up the papers she stole from my sister's escritoire. If we caught her, a promise to withdraw my prosecution against her may work wonders."

"I trust in the Lord that she and her companions may soon be brought to justice," said the clergyman. "Why else would we be here? I admit to holding a grudge. They might have ruined my friend Ernest, who is so honest that he suspects no one. He reminds me a bit of Myshkin in that Dostoyevsky novel *The Idiot*. I will remain in London a few days, and see how the search progresses."

"Dad," cried Rose, entering the apartment, "there is to be a splendid concert at St. James's Hall tonight. Do, please, let's go."

"Certainly. We will all go," laughed Frank. "I will send

64

round to the box-office and secure seats at once. Should Blake want us, we can leave word where we are to be found."

The concert-room was crowded, and on leaving it they became involved in the whirl of a fashionable crush.

Ellaby called for a cab. While they waited for it a rush from behind separated Rose from her friends.

"This way, miss," said a man to her; "the cab is waiting for you."

She followed the fellow in all simplicity, and soon she was sitting inside a soft, delicately-perfumed vehicle, which drove off at a furious rate almost as soon as she entered it.

A beautifully dressed lady sat facing her. She smiled kindly on the young and agitated girl.

"There is some mistake. I have lost my friends. Oh, pray forgive me for getting into your carriage instead of our cab. Please tell your coachman to stop," cried Rose in alarm.

"I saw your mistake and it amused me," said the lady. Rose detected a very slight accent. "I dearly love a little joke. Tell me where you wish to go to and my man shall drive us there."

"But my friends…" Rose continued.

"Will arrive after you do, and you will have the laugh against them. They deserve a taste of anxiety for losing you. The Silver Bell Hotel? I know it quite well. My house lies the same way, but it comes first.

"We will pause there for a moment, if you don't mind,

and then I will take you to your own people."

The splendor of the equipage in which she found herself and the aristocratic bearing of the white-haired lady, who patronized her with such an easy grace, were sufficient to lull all suspicion of foul play in Rose's mind.

Indeed, she felt that she was an intruder, and she considered her hostess very gracious in treating her with such good humour.

They pulled up outside a large but dismal-looking house.

"Here we are at my home," said the lady. "Come in with me, if only for a minute. No, I insist. You are too nervous to be left alone. Come! We shall yet reach the Silver Bell before your folks get there."

The door of the building opened, and by itself, it seemed. Silently it closed behind them, leaving them in a dark passage.

"Take my hand," said her conductress in a more commanding voice. "I'll lead you to the light!"

Rose began to feel frightened now, but also felt she had no choice but to follow her guide along the black corridor, down a number of steps, then to the sill open air, again into another building, and up a high flight of stairs.

"Open for us Belus—open!" said the woman.

Rose was now conscious that some creature was walking in front of them.

She could hear its breath coming and going quickly, but its footfall made no sound, and she wondered whether it was a

66

monkey or a human being.

Suddenly her eyes were blinded by a great flood of light. She stood in one of the most lavishly-furnished rooms her imagination could conceive.

She saw that Belus was a dreadfully attenuated man. His skin was dry and yellow, and his flesh all withered up like that of a mummy, to which he bore a strong resemblance. The horribleness of his appearance was increased by the fact that he had lost one eye, and was missing an arm.

These injuries were all on his left side, and they suggested that he had been involved in a terrible accident.

"Belus has been with me for many years," said the strange lady, "and he is very faithful."

"Unto death," declared the ghastly-looking man.

"It is well said," laughed his mistress. "Unto death! For now, get us coffee," she added.

"Indeed, indeed," protested Rose. "I must not stay. Do, please, let me go to my friends. They will be quite upset at my disappearance."

"We will leave here within ten minutes," said the lady, smilingly. "The coffee will revive you. I shall feel hurt if you do not take it."

It proved to be a delicious Arabian decoction, and was served in tiny gold cups chased in a most elegant way. Rose commented on drink's quality.

"A dash of salt does it," said the servant, smiling.

67

But instead of stimulating Rose it made her so drowsy that in a couple of minutes she was sound asleep on the luxurious sofa on which she sat.

Her hostess, Mrs. Dulk, stood over her and regarded with a pumpkin grin the prostrate figure. She had not left town as Polti had done. Instead she started following Rose the moment she saw her.

"Now what?" asked Belus, creeping to her side, "revenge or merely simple villainy?"

"Greed, of course" answered the woman shortly. "This girl is worth a fortune to me.

"Ah! That's the duke's knock. Take care he does not enter here. Nor must he know of this girl's presence in the house. The time is not yet ripe for the disclosure I have to make. Go to him. You may tell him that I'm here, and would see him on a matter of grave importance.

"Do my bidding well, my faithful Belus, and I will reward you."

"Yes," muttered the man, as he seemed to melt from the room, "as you did before, with the loss of an arm and an eye. Your rewards are perfect. But I have a reward for you, too."

"Ah! my beautiful Rose," reflected the woman, unable to take her eyes off her prisoner. "What is to be your fate? Are you destined for an early grave, or will you soon wear one of England's noblest coronets?"

Chapter IX

"Where's Rose?" demanded Ernest, as the three men clustered round the cab.

"She was by my side a second ago," said Ellaby.

"I spoke to her a moment ago," declared Briarton. "It's ridiculous to suppose she has lost us."

They looked in every direction. They waited till the crush had spent itself, and the pavement was fairly clear. But to their confusion they could see nothing of her.

They returned to the hall; she was not there.

The neighborhood was searched, police and cabmen questioned, but they could gain no tiding of the missing lady.

The extraordinary mystery of her disappearance appalled them. It was as though she had been suddenly swept off the face of the earth.

They made haste back to the hotel, hoping against hope, that she might have reached it first. Only disappointment awaited them.

The clergyman and Truelove were both plunged into the deepest distress and consternation. Ellaby, too, was greatly concerned. It seemed absurd that he should no sooner find the girl he had been searching for all these years than he should allow her to be snatched from him again.

"It's past all comprehension," he said, "that with three of us to guard her she should be taken in this miraculous way. It makes one believe in the supernatural. If money will bring her back she will soon be with us again. I'll offer a thousand pounds reward for her recovery. I'll send advertisements tonight to all the daily papers.

"I think you heartily for that generous decision," said Ernest, "but we must strain every nerve to find her ourselves."

"And pray fervently to the One above to bless and protect her," said Briarton. "But I have faith she'll be reunited with us before too long."

Before the missives to the newspapers could be dispatched, Sexton Blake called on them to report progress he had made hunting down the Red Lights.

Ellaby's kidnapping and the discovery of the murdered

70

body in the old mill's pool had made this a police business.

The detective listened to the story of Rose's disappearance with some surprise and rising anger.

"You're foolish, the lot of you. I warned you to stay in the hotel and out of sight. It wasn't an idle request. Well, what's done is done. I can only suppose," he said "that this is the work of your friend Madame Dulk. How she managed to accomplish her purpose so easily, and in the full blaze of Piccadilly, I do not know.

"Doubtless her object is extortion. She is determined not to let you escape her, Ellaby. If the young lady is in her power, I can promise you that I will soon bring about her release. Now that I know about this woman, it will not be long before I find her.

"However, they are an exceedingly slippery gang to deal with. For instance, I have absolute proof that Calder Dulk and Nizza Polti left King's Cross this morning by the North express, which makes its first stop at Peterborough.

"I wired to that old cathedral city to have these two people detained until I arrived and formally charged them. No one answering their descriptions was to be found in the whole train.

"Indeed, it chanced, that there was only one lady aboard, and she is the daughter of a well-known clergyman.

"Since the train goes at break-neck speed the guard was certain that no one left it *en route*, and that Nizza Polti and her

71

male companion were in their carriage when it started from King's Cross.

"They have managed to do the vanishing trick to perfection."

"If that gang has succeeded in capturing poor Rose, they hold a trump card. I dare not move against them for fear of her life. They're quite capable of using her as a shield to protect them from my vengeance."

It was Ellaby who spoke.

"That's true," Blake allowed ruefully. "But even if they escape your hostility, they have still to reckon with the police. The offer of a thousand pounds reward may bring a communication from her gang."

During this conversation, another and ever more important one was happening in the strange house whither Rose had been conveyed.

Madame Dulk had left her beautiful and unconscious prisoner still reclining on the luxurious couch.

Entering another apartment, more superbly furnished than the first, she found a tall, stoutly-built, aristocratic gentleman waiting for her. He had keen, grey eyes, which glittered under his grey, heavy eyebrows. His white hair was clipped short to his military-looking head and his moustache was well-trimmed and midnight-black.

"I received you message," he said in cold, haughty tone, "and I have come. What have you to tell me now?"

"Will your Grace not deign to take a seat?" said Dulk humbly. "The missing child is again found. Of course she has grown to be a woman now. She is beautiful, and would ornament the highest station in the land."

"Tut!" he spoke impatiently; "what an old story this is! Woman, if you are in difficulties and want money, why not tell me so, and take your chance whether I give it to you or not? Why do you always try to touch my purse by some fabrication?"

"Never, your Grace, never in my life!" she protested. "I have been mistaken before—that is all. I have never willfully deceived you. This time I have made no error. I have seen the minister who took possession of her when I was in prison. She is with him now.

"But there may be danger. Her Australian guardian's brother is here and with her. He came over expressively to find her, and to vindicate her rights. He is enormously rich, and he will spend all he is worth to establish her true identity. With my assistance he might learn this in half-an-hour.

"Now it is for your Grace's consideration whether you will submit to be compelled by law to accept this young lady as the daughter of your late elder brother, and allow her to take over the estates you now possess.

"You can arrange matters with me so that the proof of Lady Rose Fenton's existence can be forever destroyed, and she herself be removed to some safe place abroad.

"As she has never known the joys for the position she is

73

legally entitled to, she can never miss them."

The Duke of Fenton, resting his head on his hand, sat for some minutes without speaking.

"It is a hard problem to solve," he muttered. "If I had only myself to consider, this girl might take her place in our family without hindrance from me. But I doubt whether it would be good for her. One has to be bred up to the tiara to wear it with ease.

"But my son, my dear and only son! The sudden appearance of his cousin plays sad havoc with his financial position!

"What do you propose, Madame?" he added in a louder tone, and looking up sharply at her.

"I propose that you should have a few days to prosecute your own inquiries about the Rev. Briarton and his adopted daughter," was her prompt reply.

"While you are thus engaged, I will undertake to get possession of the young lady, and have her snugly housed at the big place in Bedfordshire. Then I will hand her over to you with all the proofs and documentation regarding her birth parentage, which you know I possess.

"Then it will be for you to decide what to do with her. You are already satisfied that she does exist."

"Your terms?" he repeated, waving his hand impatiently.

"Two thousand pounds."

"Set about your business," he said. And as he rose he

allowed a deep sigh to escape him.

"Remember, not a hair of her head must be injured; not a cruel word must be said to her. Do not forget that the blood of the Fentons flows in her veins. Woe betide you if you do not pay it proper respect!"

He strode from the room and out of the house, with a grand, haughty air.

At his carriage door his valet waited. The man had made such haste to be there that he was out of breath. The few words he did utter were sufficient to send the proud nobleman reeling into his equipage as though he had been stabbed in the heart.

"What can have happened?" asked Dulk, nervously.

She had followed the aristocrat to the door.

"His son is dead," said Belus, who was by her side. "His only son has been struck down suddenly in the billiard room of his club; heart disease, they said.

"So much for the pride of birth and the joy of riches! These aristocrats despise us and trample on us, but they all have to die—oh, yes, they all have to die!"

Chapter X

When Rose finally recovered her senses her brain was
dizzy and numbed and her muscles felt sore as though she had
been bruised. Heavy curtains were drawn across the windows,
and lights were still burning so she did not know whether it was
night or day.

She felt as though she had been unconscious for a long
time. Her recollection returned slowly and in a blurred, indistinct
form.

"Thank goodness, you are once more in possession or
your faculties," said Mrs. Dulk, who was sitting by her side. She
spoke with great fervor.

"Your papa has only just gone away. Do you know you have lain there like one in a trance for two days? The doctor says it is one of the most singular cases he has met with in his whole professional experience. He fancies that a small clot of blood must have gone into one of your brain's minute blood vessels, and pressing on that organ rendered you insensible.

"He advised us that once consciousness returned to you all danger would pass, and that you would be your old self again, as by a miracle. So you must rise now, and take some sustenance.

"Then I will convey you to a pretty place in the country, which your friends have taken for you, and where they are waiting for you."

The poor girl, still suffering from the effects of a powerful drug listened to these words in hopeless bewilderment.

Judging from her own feelings, had she been told that she had lain there a week she would have believed it. Now she could do nothing now but obey her hostess. What little strength she had was swallowed up in wonder.

An appetizing meal was put before her. She partook sparingly of it, yet it revived her. She was soon ready, and anxious to leave that place, hoping most devoutly that she would soon see her father.

The strange thing was when she passed out of the front door she never saw a patch of blue sky above her. Instead she walked directly into a vehicle which was waiting at the threshold, like stepping from one room into another.

A large pantechnicon van had been backed up close to the entrance right up to the door, creating made a closed-in passage from the hall of the dwelling to its interior. Generally such vehicles were used to carry furniture.

The result was that no curious eyes could see Rose leave that residence, and all view of the street was shut out from her.

A swing lamp hanging from the roof diffused a pleasant light through the interior. The floor was heavily carpeted. There was a comfortable sofa, some easy chairs; a good solid table stood towards the far end. Handy to it were lockers containing crystal, cutlery, wines and food. An oil-stove made cooking possible, and a speaking tube rendered instructions to the driver easy.

She thought it was certainly the warmest way of traveling by road that could be devised.

There were many conspicuous evidences to prove that Rose was not its first passenger. When Dulk and her prisoner had once entered the van, the driver closed the doors sharply and barred them.

The horses started off at a sharp trot.

"Now, my dear," said Dulk, decisively, "make yourself comfortable, and don't attempt any fuss, or bother me with stupid questions. You are with friends, and that is quite enough for you to know. Later you shall be told all the fine things that are in store for you."

"But," faltered poor Rose, "am I not to be taken to my father?"

"Why, of course you are! Have I not told you so? There now, amuse yourself with some of these books while I read the paper."

It was, perhaps, as well for Rose that she was too dazed just then to feel any particular alarm. It all felt like a dream, and not an entirely unpleasant one.

She attempted to read, but drowsiness assailed her, and she continued to drop into short, fitful sleeps, which seemed to tire her more than refresh her

"ROSE."

They had a comfortable lunch, for which she had but small desire, and then a cup of tea, which failed to refresh her.

On they went, keeping up a round pace. They had four good horses, and Rose fancied that these were changed at least once during one of their many short stops.

It must have been towards evening when her host herself dropped into a doze. The atmosphere of that van was close, and conducive to sleep.

Rose languidly picked the newspaper from her lap.

For some reason, which she herself cold not have

79

explained, she was pleased to see that its date was the one following the night she visited St. James's Hall. So she had *not* been unconscious for two days, as she had been told. Unless, of course, the newspaper was old. The thought made her head hurt.

Then her eyes caught sight of the advertisement offering one thousand pounds reward for her safe recovery. She then realized that her father would not be waiting for her at her destination. Still, as naïve as her *fiancée*, she did not think it possible that in law-abiding England anyone could be long detained against their will, except in a prison or a lunatic asylum.

For her own safety's sake, she determined to take things quite calmly, to show no excitement, and to obey any reasonable command she might receive.

It would require an effort to hide her anxiety and some courage to affect cheerfulness. Inside she was terrified about her captors' designs. She felt strong and brave enough to play the difficult part she had set before herself, and by enacting it well she hoped to soon escape, even if Briarton failed to find her.

The moon showered its light on them, and the stars twinkled with a frosty brightness when they at last drew up before a large, old-fashioned, substantial country house, which stood in the midst of thickly-timbered grounds and surrounded by a high wall.

The hall door was open, and in the yellow glow of the gas was seen the form of Leon Polti.

"You? Here?" cried Dulk angrily. "Why have you come

to this place?"

"I expect for the same reason as yourself!" he answered, lightly. "For safety. Everything has failed—all has gone wrong. We are all scattered like chaff before the four winds."

"Enough!" snapped the woman. "You and I will discuss business matters later. This way, my dear Rose. You will find your room has been made very comfortable for you."

"I wonder who her pretty friend is?" muttered Leon, as he threw himself on a sofa before a bright fire in one of the sitting rooms.

"The conditions of our confederation compel me to make you welcome, Leon Polti, anywhere and at any time," she said after making sure Rose was settled. "But I am sorry you are here tonight. I wish you had not come. Besides, I have done with the Red Lights forever. Some of you are clever enough men and you do great things when you work alone. But together, all you seem to do is to get in each other's way.

"I, at any rate, can afford to do without you."

"Ah," said Leon, with a cynical smile. "You have thought so before tonight. But I have some news for you—your husband is dead."

"Dead?" she echoed, starting to her feet. Then she fell back in her chair, and again repeated the dread words, "Calder Dulk is dead."

"Well, I saw Bill Bender throw him out of a quick-going train on to the rails and in a tunnel. He seemed half dead before he left us. I don't think he can possibly be alive."

"You saw this, and raised no hand to protect him?"

"I was almost insensible myself. It's a miracle I escaped the same fate. Bender believes that we played him false. He'll do his best to kill me if he ever catches me. As for being here, I won't trouble you for long. All I want is to hide for a few days. By the way, who is your young friend?"

"That, Leon Polti, is none of your business. She is worth more to me than all your abortive schemes put together would have been, even had you brought them to a successful issue. And I share with no one."

"Don't you," Leon muttered, after she had left him to his own reflections. "Let me look at that advertisement again. 'One thousand pounds reward.' Ah, a nice little sum. Yes, as far as I can judge, the description of the missing lady tallies with that of the one who has just arrived. What an odd thing they don't give her name. Some reason for it, I suppose. 'Clothes marked, R.B.—Apply Proprietor, Silver Bell Hotel.'

"It would be rather amusing were I to snatch this pleasant little prize from your grasp, Madame Dulk. I want a thousand pounds quite as much as you do. But nothing can be done till the morning, when I will contrive to get a look at the stolen beauty."

Chapter XI

A few days had passed, and to the surprise of Sexton
Blake no one had yet made any serious claim on the thousand
pounds reward so widely advertised.

Suggestions, descriptions and offers of help came from
all parts of the country, but nothing that promised the quick
return of Rose.

As Briarton and Ellaby were discussing it over one of
their gloomy breakfasts, Sexton Blake entered the dining room,
and sat down at their table.

"I have some news," he said disconsolately. "I have
found Calder Dulk."

"Good!" cried Frank, "through him we may get Rose, if his wife has had anything to do with the dear girl's disappearance."

"I fear he is past giving help to us, or to anyone. Someone else beat you to him. Dulk is dead."

"How?" asked Ellaby in a low tone.

"His body was found in a tunnel on the Great Northern Railway. It must have dropped from the North Express I told you he and Nizza Politi took tickets by.

"He might have fallen out by accident, or he might have committed suicide; but both these theories are negated by the fact that his throat bears the impress of a powerful thumb and finger. They may have exercised sufficient pressure to throttle him."

"Surely Nizza Polti had not

"ERNEST TRUELOVE." enough strength—"

"Dear me, no. Indeed, it seems pretty clear that there never was any sister, and that is how I and Scotland Yard have been so often tricked on to wrong scents. Leon and Nizza are one.

"I managed at Peterborough to get permission to examine all the luggage that had come by that particular train,

84

and which had been left in the cloak room.

"This chanced to consist of one petite portmanteau. It contained a regularly built-up woman's costume, such as are used by female impersonators on the stage, only more delicately manufactured, to suit a drawing-room. The wig was a work of art. *Now* I understand why no Nizza could be found in that train. Leon had entered it a King's Cross as a girl, and had left it at Peterborough in his proper male attire.

"I don't understand," said Ellaby. "He boarded the train as a woman, and exited as a man. Why would he leave his luggage behind?"

"Good question. I assume because he couldn't claim his luggage as a man, and was in a hurry to leave the station. He must have multiple changes of dresses and wigs.

"But to continue, it turns out, too, that a man answering the description of the fellow who left you to starve at the water-mill jumped into the carriage in which Polti and Dulk were, just as the train was on the move.

"Bill Bender." said Ellaby. "There is not a worse ruffian unhanged. I suppose he and Dulk quarreled and Bender strangled him, and then threw him on the line."

"Indeed," said Blake. "But it's not clear how Polti survived. So far the murderer has made good his escape. But the police are keen after him all over the country, and after the whole gang.

"Polti would not be foolish enough to return to the city

soon. In his absence I think we shall see a quick extinction of the Red Lights of London."

"Well, you were right about Dulk and Polti working together, so you may be right about that."

Ernest Truelove just then returned from an early lecture at his college. But his mind was too much stirred with anxiety over Rose to have benefitted from it.

"I suppose you have no news of Miss Briarton?" His tone was one of reproach and hopelessness. The grief which he could never escape gave his face a dour expression.

"You are wrong, Mr. Truelove, this time," said the detective, with a faint smile. "I bring you great news. No less the personage than the Duke of Fenton himself shall restore Miss Rose Briarton to you." To the Vicar he added, "Perhaps, my dear sir, you will read that letter, and out loud."

He handed an envelope to the astonished clergyman, who opened it and repeated its contents:

"Rev. and Dear Sir,—

"We, as solicitors to the Duke of Fenton, are instructed by his Grace to ease your anxiety as to the welfare of the young lady to whom you have so kindly acted as guardian for some years past.

"He believes that it is within his power to being about her return to you with little or no delay.

"With this view he desires that you meet him at our

86

offices today at 12 o'clock, when he trusts to be in a position to discuss with you this young lady's real position in society, and her prospects, with more freedom than is consistent with such a purely professional communication as this.

"We are, Rev. and Dear Sir,

"Your obedient Servants,

"Martindale & Co."

"What does this mean?" Mr. Briarton, wondered, "and what can the Duke of Fenton have to do with my Rose?"

"Simply and briefly," said Sexton Blake, "the facts seem to be these: Martindale and I were schoolboys together at Winchester, and knowing I had this matter in hand, he confided the true state of affairs to me last night.

"It is clear that the late Duke of Fenton (the present duke's elder brother), was a somewhat adventuresome young man. During his travels in Australia he fell in love with, and married a lady who had everything to recommend her except birth and fortune.

"He persuaded her to keep the union a secret until he had at least seen his parents, and had endeavoured to win their countenance to this wedding of wealth with poverty. The ship he sailed in from Melbourne unhappily sank, and he, with many others, drowned.

"His wife lodged with your sister, Mr. Ellaby, and in her house she died suddenly before she could know her husband's sad fate.

"I need not tell you how Miss Ellaby left the child to your care, or how the papers establishing her right to the title of Lady Fenton excited the Dulks. I have ascertained that during their voyage home husband and wife quarreled.

"It was the present duke who got Madame sentenced to imprisonment for endeavouring to obtain money under false pretenses.

"She produced the child, but at the critical moment her husband went off with the documents necessary to establish her identity. In fact, it was the usual criminal bungle.

"But though the duke, for his own protection, sent this woman to gaol, he quite believed her tale, and when she was released he had some other transaction with her, for she was then able to produce the documents he had so much wanted before.

"She and her husband had now come to some sort of agreement again.

"When the duke heard that Rose had really been found anew, he allowed this woman to secure her. He wavered between his good impulses and his bad ones.

"He had not made up his mind what to do about his niece, when his only son was suddenly struck down. Any reason to hide her identity died with his son. The duke has taken this catastrophe as a warning from above, and he has now resolved to freely recognize Lady Rose Fenton, and to accord her the revenues and privileges which are her due.

"So, if you please, we will hasten on to Hanover Square, and keep this appointment with Messsrs. Martindale and Co. Why, gentlemen, you don't look just as delighted as you should with my great news."

"Firstly, we still don't know where she is. Secondly, it seems," said Briarton, "that if we do recover Rose it will be but to lose her at once in the turmoil of fashionable life."

"A medical student can scarcely aspire to the hand of a duke's daughter," said Ernest, in a crestfallen way.

"I could have given her as much money as she could ever reasonably spend," muttered Frank Ellaby.

"Nonsense!" cried Sexton Blake. "If the young lady is worth troubling about at all she will be just as good, and as lovable, bearing a title as if she remained a simple miss.

"I can't understand how it is," the detective grumbled, "but I get more dismayed when I give people good news than when I give to them the bad. It's the detective's lot to always be received in the opposite way from that which he has a right to expect."

Shortly afterwards they left the house but did not go far. They were soon stopped by the hoarse cries of newspaper vendors and their barking:

"SUIDICE OF THE DUKE OF FENTON!"

It was true. The untimely death of his much-loved son had driven the nobleman to this rash act.

"We are as far from finding Rose as ever," groaned

Briarton.

"I fear so," said Mr. Blake, "his lawyers know nothing at all concerning her whereabouts. If the duke knows, he didn't tell them."

On their return to the hotel, the priest was informed that a rough-looking man was waiting in the minister's sitting room to see him, and that he had some very important information for them.

They all went up, but it chanced that Frank Ellaby was the first to enter the apartment.

"What!" he cried, recognizing the burly figure standing defiantly with his back to the window. "More unbelievable good luck! I'm glad you've come home, Bill Bender!"

Cracked rib or not, he would have made a spring on his old gaoler, but Bender seized a heavy cut-glass water bottle which was near at hand, and raising it high above his head, cried:

"Move a step, and I'll brain you!"

Sexton Blake, who had followed Frank in, caught the situation with a glance.

He made a dart round through another room onto the balcony outside. Springing through the window of Briarton's room, he caught Bill from behind and had him on the floor before that powerful gentleman was aware of his presence.

At the same moment Ernest Truelove sprang to the detective's help.

"Don't kill me!" gasped Bill, "you'll never forgive

yourselves if you do. I've got a message—a message from the young lady—from Miss Rose Briarton!"

Chapter XII

Leon Polti's intention of delivering Rose to her family,
receiving the reward and baulking Madame Dulk's well-laid
plans would have succeeded but for one thing. During his
morning ramble through the grounds he detected Bill Bender
skulking among the trees. He must have climbed over the wall.

A feeling of cold terror struck him, for he knew well this
desperate character had only one purpose in being there: to kill
him. The latter was sure that so far Bill had not seen him—had,
indeed, only guessed that he might be there. So he crept quickly
back to the house, resolved to remain in hiding until his enemy
should grow tired of watching.

He had one consolation, and it was that while Bill lay
waiting for them outside, Madame Dulk would not dare to
venture out to set her schemes in motion either.

"It's a bitter reflection that I should be caged up here and
powerless to denounce my husband's murderer, when he might
be so easily taken," declared the lady angrily after he told her
what he saw.

"All might have gone well had we left this Frank Ellaby
alone. The unlucky plot emanated from you and your husband.
Now the hue and cry is out after us hot and active," said Leon.

"Puh! I have no fear of that. What can they prove against
me?"

"Sufficient to send you into penal servitude for life. The
sooner we are both out of the country the better."

"True. But your way shall not be mine. I have some little
business to settle, and that accomplished I shall be able to take
care of myself in future."

"That is exactly my case," muttered Leon to himself,
"and both our interests revolve around that young girl."

Aloud he added, "So long as Bill remains on guard
outside we are powerless to do anything."

"If you were a man, you would go out and kill him," she
said contemptuously.

"And attract the attention of the police to this, our only
remaining refuge? No, thanks, all we can do is to wait."

"Coward. He's inside the wall, no one would know and

93

you could buy him on the grounds," she said.

He ignored her.

Polti was not the only one who had seen Bill Bender lurking in those woods. Rose, at first, much to her alarm, had encountered him in one of her brief walks, and promising him rich rewards, had persuaded him to take her message to Mr. Briarton, at the Silver Bell Hotel. It was impossible for her to scale the barrier.

Bill's surprise at finding himself face to face with Frank Ellaby was almost spiritual. "Now, look here," said the desperado, when they allowed him to regain his feet. They had securely bound his hands. "If you want to rescue that young lady, I know where she is, and I will take you to her. But you'll have to let me go scot free afterwards. And I want the reward, of course. If you can't agree to those terms, my lips will remain closed for ever, and you all can croak before I'll give you any help."

"Remember, Bill," said Blake, "we aren't the police, and we can't control them. Take us to where Miss Rose Briarton is confined, and we will give you the money and your freedom right enough; but you will have to take your chance as to whether the police get you or not."

"That's a chance I take every day," growled the ruffian. "Come on, I'm your man. But not one of you must leave my sight. I'm not giving you any information except this: The place lies between Bedford and St. Neots. It won't take long to get there by train."

They reached their destination in due course. Rather than rush in they stayed outside the main gate and staked it out.

Hours passed. Eventually the park-like gates of the principal drive opened, and Polti, closely muffed up, emerged into the high road. He was alone and in a smart gig to which was harnessed a strong, spirited horse. After he noticed that Bill had left the grounds he ventured to leave.

At the sight of Bender he uttered a cry of dismay, and slashed the beast in front of him unmercifully.

But there was no escape for him! He cursed the fates he so recently praised. With a roar like that of a tiger Bill sprang on to the back of the vehicle. Somehow he managed to free his hands. By sheet muscular strength he dragged his heavy body up on to the seat by the side of the driver.

The two men immediately began grappling.

The tugging and jerking of the reins, the swaying of the gig and the dreadful mutterings of the combatants maddened the high-spirited horse. Getting the bit between its teeth, it tore madly forward, blind to all before it.

"See!" cried Ernest, in a tone of horror, "where the road takes a sudden bend it skirts a cutting, which makes a sheer drop of forty feet into a turbulent stream. The animal's spooked. Will it hold to the highway, or go over?"

Not until the horse reached the edge of the cutting did it realize its danger. With a sudden jerk it turned, as if to get back

95

to the highway and safety once more.

The jerk caused the shafts to snap off short, and the traces which held the horse were torn in two. The animal regained its footing, but the gig went over the awful height.

And still they struggled while they were descending to their doom. They disappeared down the deadly chasm into the deep, fast-running water.

When they were found it was seen that in the descent the carriage had flipped completely over, and had buried Leon and Bill under it at the bottom of the stream. They had no chance of swimming for their lives, even if they were conscious when they reached the water.

The action had been witnessed from one of the upper windows of the mansion by Mrs. Dulk. Except that the horror of it fascinated her for but a moment, and it occasioned her no regret. She turned away with a shrug of her shoulders.

The telegram she held in her hand concerned her more deeply. It told her of the suicide of the Duke of Fenton and urged her to meet the sender of it at St. Neots that night.

It was signed by Belus.

"So the duke has gone," she thought, "and with him my last hope of immediate wealth and safety. The documents proving the legitimacy of Rose are still in my possession, and should be valuable. But I dare not offer them to Frank Ellaby and to Mr. Briarton. It would be one more crime to the list they have against me.

"They had best be destroyed. They'll never benefit any person but myself for I have gone through much to secure and retain them."

From her traveling bag she withdrew a packet of papers. In the act of casting them into the fire, she paused.

"Even yet they may be of service," she reflected.

At that moment she heard the voice of Frank Ellaby and the others, as they ascended the principal stairs.

"The end has come! They're here to take me!" she ejaculated in terror. "But they shall never have these precious proofs."

The documents she had sinned so deeply to obtain she cast to the burning coal, and the flames greedily devoured them.

The voices came nearer and nearer. But instead of opening her door they passed the room, and next she heard a joyous cry from Rose, as she was once again in the clergyman's embrace and her lover's glad welcome.

Quickly and silently Dulk ran into her bedroom. Seizing her cloak and hat, and securing her valuables, she crept down the back staircase, out of the house, through a back gate for which she had the key and on to the free road.

She met Belus at St. Neots that evening. To her dismay he was accompanied by a pair of police inspectors, who very adroitly decorated her wrists with handcuffs and conveyed her straight to the London train, which was already in the station. The two officers from Scotland Yard informed her that they had secured sufficient evidence against her to warrant any judge to send her back to prison for fifteen years.

"When you in your fury threw that lamp at me, and burned half my body away, I swore to be revenged on you," cried Belus, who had accompanied them to the station and now thrust an evil face into the carriage window.

"And my time has come now. Take her away, gentlemen—take her away and to Hell with her!"

With a scream of satisfaction the engine dashed forward, and was soon lost in the darkness of the night.

##

Frank Ellaby, being in doubt as to what he should do with his wealth, showered most of it on Rose and Ernest, who in a few months' time were to marry.

"I did the best I could for you in the matter," Blake afterwards said to Ellaby; "but it was not so much as I wished."

"Thank goodness!" said the Rev. Briarton, "we have been the means of suppressing those terrible people, the Red Lights of London."

"Yes," agreed Frank; "we have managed to clear away four desperate criminals at least."

Although Frank, Ernest and the vicar knew about Rose's true identity, they decided to keep it secret for their own benefit since they didn't want to lose her. Besides, they had no proof.

To his relief, Sexton Blake was so well-rewarded he would not have to worry about money for many years. He and

Gervaise became partners and Blake planned to move to better offices.

"Think of it," he told his French friend. "Just a few short days ago I feared I would have to shutter my business and sell meat pies for a living. That's how quick fortune can turn. Now I see a bright future ahead. There's no stopping me now. By the time I'm finished only Sherlock Holmes himself will garner more respect. Just watch. I'm going to create a dynasty, Jules, from this humble beginning."

THE END

COMPLETE BOOK

By HAL MEREDETH.

THE MISSING MILLIONAIRE

The Story of a Daring Detective.

"And still they struggled, though they were descending to their doom."

The "HALFPENNY MARVEL"

No. 6

A·NEW·BOOK·EVERY·WEDNESDAY
22 WHITEFRIARS ST. LONDON E·C

100

The Missing Millionaire

by

Harold Blyth

CHAPTER I.

The Detective and His Visitor—A Strange Story of Treachery—
The Missing Millionaire!

"Mr. Frank Ellaby wishes to see you, sir,"

"Good!" answered Mr. Sexton Blake. "Let him come up,
and at once."

The clerk withdrew, and his master gazed thoughtfully at
the grimy window of his office in New Inn Chambers.

"So," he muttered, "my wealthy client has come at last,
thanks to the influence of my friend Gervaise, of Pairs. I wonder
what kind of mission it is he has in hand that is to bring me in
such high rewards! Gervaise says it may keep me busy for a year

or two."

Sexton Blake belonged to the new order of detectives. He possessed a highly-cultivated mind which helped to support his active courage. His refined, clean-shaven face readily lent itself to any disguise, and his mobile features assisted to clinch any facial illusion he desired to produce.

The door again opened, and a tall, handsome man, whose cheeks were bronzed by travel, and whose grey eyes were large and prominent, entered.

"Mr. Blake, I believe?" he said, as he paused on the threshold.

"Very much at your service, Mr. Frank Ellaby. Pray take a seat, and let me hear what I can do for you. Mr. Gervaise prepared me for a visit from you, but I am quite in the dark as to the nature of the business you desire me to undertake."

"It will prove more troublesome than dangerous," said the visitor, with a slight smile. "I will tell you my story, and then you will understand exactly what I want.

"My sister and myself were left orphans before we had finished our schooling. Some friends sent her out to Australia, where I believe she obtained a comfortable situation. It is unnecessary for me to bore you with a description of my struggles for existence. When I was about twenty I, like thousands of other men, old and young, took a severe attack of gold fever. I was determined to get to the Antipodes by hook or by crook, and try my luck at the diggings. If I came across my sister, well and good, although I did not start with any design of finding her. I had one object in view, and one only—that was wealth!

"I have obtained my desire," he added, with a heavy sigh, "but my heart is empty, and my life desolate!

"Out in Australia I met a man and his wife, with whom I became so friendly that he and I became partners in a claim, at which we toiled for months without finding one grain of gold. He was some years older than myself, and he went by the name of Calder Dulk. I don't suppose it was his real title, for I know now that there was nothing true about him.

"In those days I would have trusted him with my life. He, again, was younger than his wife, who was a tall, majestic woman, of French extraction, wonderfully accomplished, fiercely ambitious, and altogether unscrupulous.

"I always mistrusted her, and, unfortunately, I had not the art to conceal my dislike.

"Just when we were despairing of ever having any luck, and were thinking of seeking our fortune in some other part, we struck a rich vein of the precious ore, and found ourselves wealthy.

"Like many before us, this sudden success turned our heads. Nothing would do but we must hasten to Melbourne and enjoy ourselves.

"A few days after we arrived there I accidentally found the house where my sister lived. I got there just in time to bid her good-bye for ever. She was dying. A beautiful, golden haired girl of perhaps four years of age was playing in the room.

"'Frank' gasped my sister, 'I swore to the mother of little Rose there, when *she* lay on *her* deathbed, that I would protect her child until she came of age. Take the same oath to me, Frank, so that I may die in peace.'

"There was, of course, no refusing this request at that awful moment, so I most solemnly took the vow she wished.

"'In that cabinet, standing in the corner over there, you will find some papers which will explain who her parents were,' my sister continued, speaking with great difficulty, for life's lamp was at its last flicker. 'When you have perused them you will understand how precious she is, and how important it is that she is well guarded till she becomes a woman and can claim her own!'

"As she ceased speaking, she pressed my hand in hers. Smiling on me, she passed into the eternal sleep.

"This sad event so distressed me that I could do nothing in connection with the child or anything just then. Calder Dulk led me away from the place to the hotel where we were staying. He advised me to remain alone and keep quiet until the morning, which I did.

"When the morrow came both he and his wife had disappeared, and they had taken every ounce of gold I possessed with them! Nor was this all. They had run off with the child, too, not forgetting to secure the papers relating to her birth, to which

105

my sister attached so much importance.

"I need not tell you what my emotions were under this stinging reversal of my fortune, at this horrible breach of faith, and at my inability to keep the oath I had so recently made to my dying sister.

"I was powerless to follow them, for I had not sufficient money even to pay the hotel bill. There was nothing I could do but return to the diggings, and by hard labour again woo the favour of the goddess of chance.

"I swore then in my heart that, if I ever did attain wealth, I would spend every farthing of it, if necessary, in hunting down the traitor who had betrayed me, and in finding the child who was so infamously stolen from my protection! So, Mr. Sexton Blake, I am here to obtain you co-operation in this search, which must never cease till my end is attained!"

"How long is it since this double robbery was committed?" asked the detective.

"Fourteen years."

"Whew! That's a long time. Dulk and his wife may be dead; the girl has become a woman—"

"And a beautiful one, too, I am sure. You see," Mr. Ellaby explained, "for a long, long time my luck was so bad I scarcely succeeded in keeping body and soul together. It is only recently that the wheel of fortune has taken a turn. Then, as always happens, gold poured in on me till I was tired of gathering it."

"Have you heard anything of these people since?"

"Absolutely nothing. But your friend, Gervaise, of Paris, believes that Madame Dulk has visited the French capital quite recently. While there she plundered the aristocracy in a most grand and daring manner. No one answering the description of her husband was seen to visit her. As she has undoubtedly left France, it is surmised that she is either in England or America."

"A very wide address," said Blake, with a smile. "If she is a high-toned adventuress, and is in London, she will be easily found. But you are giving me a tall order. When Stanley was sent to Africa to find Livingstone, his search was at least limited to *one* continent. The whole world is before *me*. But I will do my best—"

"Do that, and whether you fail or succeed, you shall have your own reward. Day and night I shall be at your service to aid you, and you may direct me as you choose."

"We will work together, and I can promise you heartiness on my part. But I fear if we find Calder Dulk that I shall have helped to being about a murder."

It was the detective who spoke.

"What do you mean?" demanded Ellaby.

"Simply this: you wish to meet him, *so that you may kill him!*"

"When I get him will be time enough for me to decide what I shall do with him," replied the other. "I know you cannot give me any useful advice off-hand. I must let you have a little time to digest my story. Meanwhile, will you lunch with me? I have been away from England so long that it will be safer for both of us if I trust to you to select the restaurant."

"With pleasure," said Blake. "Let us stroll as far as Charing Cross. I think best when I am walking. Come round this way," he added, when they stood in Wych Street, and he pointed to St. Clement's Danes. "I must give a minute's call in Arundel Street."

Two other men were watching them from a neighboring doorway. They took great care not to be seen.

"That's our man," said one to the other, indicating Frank Ellaby. "Once we secure him we shall be as well off as anyone need ever want to be. He's worth millions! You shadow him, Scooter, and make no mistake about it. If you let him give you the slip it will be as much as your skin is worth."

"You may as well come with me!"

"No thanks," laughed the first speaker. "That job is not in my way at all."

In the narrowest part of the Strand, between the two churches, the detective and Frank Ellaby became separated in the roadway, and by some evil chance the latter was knocked down and run over by a carelessly driven hansom cab.

He was carried to the opposite pavement in an insensible condition.

Mr. Sexton Blake feared that he was killed outright.

A tall, handsome woman pressed her way through the

crowd, which at once surrounded the injured man.

Her hair was as white as snow, and her eyes were coal-black in color. It was a face time had treated tenderly. It was determined and commanding, too.

"Let your friend be brought to my house," she said to Blake. "It is close here—only round the corner in Norfolk Street. He may die before he can be taken to the hospital. A doctor lives opposite to where I reside."

Gratefully indeed did the detective accept this opportune proposal. Apart altogether from the common sympathies of humanity, which were strongly developed in Blake, he had selfish reasons for desiring to keep this exceedingly wealthy client alive.

It happened, fortunately, so that the front apartment leading off the hall, in the Norfolk Street house, was a bedroom, and here they laid the unconscious man.

In a few minutes Dr. Tuppy, from opposite, was by his side making a careful examination of his injuries.

"One rib fractured," he said. "Severe scalp wounds. No danger. Quiet, good nursing and my advice will soon put him on his feet again. He must not, on any account, be removed for some days. I don't know, madame—"

He paused to be supplied with the name of the lady who had called him.

"Vulpino," she said in a musical voice.

"Well, I don't know, Madame Vulpino, whether you can

109

possibly allow the gentleman to stay in your rooms, but I can assure you that he can only be conveyed out of them, at present, at the risk of his life."

"I would not turn an injured dog from my roof," said madame, with a touch of emotion. "He shall stay here till he can be taken away with safety. I have an elderly woman with me who will nurse him—"

"Excellent," said the doctor.

"Believe me, he shall want for nothing."

"You are indeed a good Samaritan, madame," declared Blake. "My friend is a man of means, and any expense you may be put to—"

She closed his speech with a proud wave of her hand, which clearly indicated that she would not accept any money recompense for the inconvenience she was putting herself to.

"Now, my dear sir," said Dr. Tuppy, "you can do nothing more for your friend. He is in excellent hands. I will see the nurse, and give her my instructions. He will soon recover consciousness, and then he must have absolute quietness. Of course, you may come round in the morning and see how he is."

Blake, quite easy in his mind, left his new client in the house in Norfolk Street, and set about a careful consideration of the problem which had been put before him, and attending to such other matters as he had in hand.

The next day, at ten o'clock, he called to see how Ellaby was progressing.

The door was opened by a typical specimen of the London lodging-house "slavey."

"Well," he said, good humouredly, "how is my friend this morning?"

"Wot friend? Oh, the gent as was ill yesterday? He's gone."

"Gone! Impossible! How did he go?"

"That's just what missis says when a lodger gets out without paying what he owes. Why, sir, how can I tell you how they goes?"

"Madme Vulpino is in, I suppose?" said the detective, as he tried to persuade himself that the girl was talking foolishly, and at random.

"She has gone too," was the answer. "That was her room he was taken into. Her time was up last night, and she went, and paid up, too. She gave me half-a-crown, and told me not to bother her when she was getting her luggage into the cab. So I didn't. I just went to sleep in the kitchen. My missis was out at the time."

"Will you let me look into Madame Vulpino's room?" said Blake, more perplexed than ever detective was yet.

"Why, of course I will, sir," laughed the girl. "You can come and live in it if you like to pay the rent regular, and gas, and coals, and boots is hextra, and I does the boots."

There was no doubt about it. Frank Ellaby was not in the house, nor could any information be obtained as to how he had

111

left it. To make matters worse, no one knew anything about Madame Vulpino.

As for Dr. Tuppy, he simply shrugged his shoulders.

"You re all strangers to me," he said. "And I only know three things about you. First, you call me from my lunch in a dreadful hurry. Second, the removal of the patient last night was quite against my instructions, and will probably kill him. Third, I have received no fee!"

"Frank Ellaby has fallen into bad hands," thought Sexton Blake, as he made his way to his office, feeling very vexed with himself. "Not only into bad hands, but I fear, powerful ones. I must try and rescue him, whatever it costs me. There can be little doubt that he has been followed from Australia by some desperate gang, who know how wealthy he is , They have succeeded in capturing him the simplest way possible. They have him in their power, while he is quite helpless. It means a race now between my brains and another London mystery, and I'll back myself to win!"

CHAPTER II.

Frank Ellaby Finds Himself Bound and Helpless in a Cab—At the Old Water Mill

To keep the events in this remarkable history abreast of one another as much as possible, we will leave the detective to make his own way of discovering the whereabouts of his rich client and concern ourselves with Mr. Frank Ellaby's own movements.

When he regained his senses he found that he was gagged, and bound hand and foot.

He was in some kind of vehicle which carried no lights. As it jolted along a rough, dark road, it rattled like a ramshackle

113

old four-wheeler. He was stretched along it from the back to the front seat. A piece of plank covered the space between, and gave him additional support.

His injuries occasioned him great pain. At present his senses were numbed, as though the effects of some powerful drug were still clinging to him. He dimly recalled the accident which had befallen him. From then to now was a blank.

He consoled himself at first with the thought that he was being conveyed to some infirmary where he would find ease, and receive kind treatment. But if this was the intention of those who had placed him in the cab, why was he gagged and bound?

The air grew keener, and the part through which they passed more and more silent, till Frank judged that they must now be in the open country. Suddenly the vehicle pulled up with a jerk which nearly sent the injured man to its other side.

"Wake up, my beauty," said a rough voice.

The door of the cab opened, and Frank's body was prodded playfully with a heavy bludgeon

"We have reached our destination. You must try and walk into our picturesque country retreat, for you are a bit too heavy for me to carry."

By the aid of the bright moon Ellaby saw that the gaunt, spectral building which stood before him and back from the road in murky ugliness had been a water-mill.

The big wheel was there yet, dripping with slimy weeds. The moon's rays made the still water look green and murderous.

114

The house itself was as forbidding structure as it is easy to imagine.

The door of the evil place opened. A man carrying a lantern emerged and came towards them. He wore a mask. His voice appeared familiar to Frank, though, at that moment, he could not identify it.

"Is it all right, Bill Bender?" he asked, addressing the rough driver.

"Quite right. Now, my young swell, I'll just undo the strap which holds your legs, and with a little support from me, you will be able to walk inside. Why, bless me, if you haven't got a lively gold lever, as big as a turnip, and a chain strong enough to hold a horse. I'll take care these trifles for you, and if you want any civility from me, you had better make no fuss about this little incident.

"You see," continued the ruffian, "if I have any of your nonsense I can give you a touch with *this*"—and he tapped the prisoner's head with a life-preserver—"or you can have a dose of *this*."

He produced a pistol and the barrel gleamed in the moonlight.

"But there," he added, with a coarse laugh, "it won't be any good for you to try on anything. We are a thousand miles from everywhere, as the saying is, and if you try to escape, all you will find will be a watery grave."

They had removed Frank's gag now. Although he was in

115

great pain he addressed them with the utmost coolness and assurance.

"I am too ill and weak to make any attempt to escape, especially from any place which promises warmth, rest, and shelter. Pray help me in, and let me lie down"

"We have ventured to take a few liberties with you tonight," said the man who wore the mask, "but we do not contemplate treating you with violence. To-morrow, however, will show us whether you are a reasonable, or an unreasonable, man—whether we must resort to force or not."

"To-morrow will be time enough for that or any other discussion. To-night my pain is so great I can hardly stand. I beg you to take me indoors. The man who guards me to-night will have an easy task."

"I am glad to see you take matters so coolly. You shall have all the attention this place affords. Let me warn you. You are as far from human aid here as though you were in your tomb."

CHAPTER III.

A Threat of Torture—Left to Starve to Death.

"How is your patient getting on now?" The man who had worn the mask asked this question of the ruffian he had called "Bill Bender."

The former was sitting before a well-spread table, enjoying a hearty meal, and the latter had just returned from the room which was to prove Frank Ellaby's prison.

"Beautiful!" was the answer. "I never saw a man in his position take things so cool and comfortable. He could not be more contented in his own hotel"

"I'd rather he made a fuss. He'll prove all the more

troublesome to us in the end. These calm, determined men are more difficult to deal with than excitable people."

"We can soon knock the nonsense out of him. What made you cover up your face with that mask to-night, Mr. Calder Dulk?"

"Why, you see," came the slow answer, "after he has paid his ransom, I don't want it to be in his power to take proceedings against me when he is once more free."

"When he is once more free?" repeated Bender, with a low chuckle. "You don't mean that he ever shall get free? Once you have got his money, he will only be a danger to you alive. *He'll have to go where the rest have gone.*"

"I neither contemplate, nor do I recommend, violence," said Dulk, with a queer look in his eyes; "when we obtain possession of the cash I shall leave him here, and you can do what you like with him."

"Thanks; and I shan't forget to keep my eyes on you, either," muttered the rascal.

Frank was put into a comfortable bed in a warm room, and he was well supplied with everything in the way of nourishment he could desire.

He felt that whoever had bandaged his injuries had done the work with some skill.

There was no window to the apartment, and all escape from it was prevented by an iron-bound oaken door, which was secured by bolts and an iron bar on the outside.

Except for the fact that he was a prisoner in that sinister building, and probably in imminent peril of his life, he might have felt as contented there as in any other place he could have been taken to.

After a long and grave consideration of his present position, he came to the unjust conclusion that Mr. Sexton Blake had proved a scoundrel, and for his own ends had made him a prisoner.

"Yes," thought Frank, 'it must be Blake. Not another soul in London knows who I am, or what I am worth! I wonder how much he will want to set me free? I wonder whether I shall ever yield to his infamous demands! I think not. He has played a dangerous game, and he shall suffer for it, unless they kill me outright. He could not have planned the accident which befell me, but my helplessness may have suggested this cunning plot. Opportunity is the great tempter. I suppose to-morrow my gaolers will tell me their intentions."

When he awoke on the following day, he felt refreshed, and so hungry, that he looked forward eagerly for the appearance of breakfast.

Frank had a remarkably strong constitution, which travel, hardship, and exposure had hardened, and not shattered.

In spite of Doctor Tuppy's prognostications, his sudden and queer removal had not retarded his recovery. He felt in himself that a few days would see him on his feet again, and in fair health.

119

His only visitor the next day was "Bill Bender."

He brought a jug of coffee and a couple of slices of bread and butter.

"We are not going to feed you up with high-class food," said the man, "because it might fire your blood, and we mean to keep you nice and cool."

This fare, rough as it proved, was very welcome to Frank.

"Now," continued the ruffian, drawing a packet of papers from his pocket, "I'm going to leave these things with you for your careful and best consideration. One is a cheque on the London Joint Stock Bank for twenty thousand pounds. Oh, my fine millionaire! we've got friends in Paris, who told us which was your London bank."

"Gervaise, of course," Frank thought; "he has planned this with Sexton Blake. I have plunged my head right into the hornet's nest."

"All you have to do," continued "Bill Bender," with a grin, "is to sign this cheque, and then, in case you should not have so much cash as that at the bank, here's a little power of attorney for you to put your name to. It authorizes Mr. Cornelius Brown to realize on any stocks or shares, bonds or certificates, personal or real estate, you may possess. Once you have signed these different documents, and we have secured what we have justly earned, you will be free to leave this place and enjoy yourself as you may think best. So it just rests with you, Mr.

Frank Ellaby, how long you remain here. We can wait for years, if necessary. *You have not one living person on earth likely to trouble themselves whether you are alive or dead!"*

How true this was Frank knew only too well, and to his sorrow.

"I can't prevent you from leaving the papers here," he said quietly; "but I will never sign one of them as long as I live!"

"That's what you think now, but we will make you change your mind soon."

"I should be a fool to sign."

Frank spoke carelessly. "So long as you want my authorization to those papers, you will keep me alive for the gratification of your own greed; but once that is satisfied, it will not matter to you whether I am alive or dead. While I am alive I have hope."

"Well, I never thought of that! How clever you are! But, look here; this matter has been put into my hands, and I am going to work it off quick. I don't suppose you are a bit more frightened of death than I am; but there's something worse than that, *and it's torture.* If you won't come to any reasonable terms, *I'll starve you into submission!* Do you hear?"

"You cur!" said Frank, contemptuously. "Why, you would run a mile from me, if I had my strength, and we were on equal terms. As it is, I'll bring you to the earth!"

On a little table by the bedside the man had placed a metal inkpot and a pen, with the papers to which he wished

Frank to put his signature.

The prisoner seized this pewter inkstand, and hurled it with all the force he could command, full in the face of his brutal custodian.

The blow was unexpected, and Bill dropped to the ground like log of wood.

Frank thought that the moment of his escape had come, and he tried to struggle into his clothes.

Alas! He was so weak that he had to sink on to the bed, and cling to it, trembling from the effects of his recent exertions.

This gave "Bill Bender" time to regain his feet, and he soon had his prisoner back between the sheets.

"So that's a sample of temper, is it?" snarled Bill. "I shall look out for you in the future. You take my advice. Sign those papers while you have a chance. I'm a bit of a rough to deal with when I'm put out, and you have marked my figure-head for life. Until those papers are signed you don't get bite nor sup from me."

With a curse Bill left Frank Ellaby to recover from his prostration as best he could.

For two days Frank had neither food nor drink given him.

In one way he suffered terribly, but this heroic treatment helped his injuries to heal up in a miraculously short space of time.

He then began to consider whether, after all, he had not

better attach his signature to the documents which were still at the side of his bed.

If he did not do the bidding of the wretches, it was certain they would starve him to death!

Circumstanced as he was he could lose nothing by agreeing to their terms. If he ever did get free he promised himself that he would punish Mr. Gervaise, of Paris, and Mr. Sexton Blake, of London, most severely for their villainy. He hoped, too, that he would be able to make them disgorge the money they had wrenched from him.

Little did he imaging that both these wrongly suspected gentlemen were at that very moment doing all they could to find and rescue him!

The next time "Bill Bender" put his head into the room, with the question whether his prisoner had come to his senses yet, Frank Ellaby said—

"I have signed all you wished me to. Bring me something to eat and drink. When you have got your money I suppose you will see that I am release from here?"

"Not much," said Bill, with a coarse laugh, as he thrust the papers into the breast pocket of his heavy overcoat. "Now, listen to me. If you had not been so obstinate, I would have done fair and honest by you. But you've been pig-headed, and you've kept me from my pleasures and enjoyments. More than that, you have marked my face. The consequence of which is that *I'm going to leave you here to starve. You can't escape. No one can come to you. Here you shall remain and slowly starve to death.*"

With this speech the ruffian left the room, bolting and barring the door behind him.

"He tells the truth for once," groaned Frank, "there is no help or hope for me. I see nothing before me but a dragging out of an existence which will be torture till the end of its last thread!"

CHAPTER IV.

Gervais, of Paris, Appears on the Scene—The "Red Lights" of
London—The Newspaper Boy's Story—Finding the Old Mill—
Dragging the Pool—Discovery of a Body.

"So far all my searchings have been in vain. I have failed
to find any trace of Mr. Frank Ellaby."

So said Sexton Blake to his fellow-worker, Detective
Gervaise, of Paris, to whom he had telegraphed directly it
became known that the millionaire had disappeared.

"I blame myself very much for this catastrophe," said
Gervaise, gloomily. "I should have described that woman to you,
and have put you on your guard against her. She was as anxious
to secure Ellaby as he was to find and punish her. She wanted me

125

to shadow him before he called on me to get information concerning her. I intended coming to England, to put you on her track, and I calculated that your speedy discovery of her would bring a substantial reward from our wealthy friend. You have already guessed that this Madame Vulpino and Mrs. Calder Dulk is one person. This unfortunate accident has played havoc with my plans. Fate seems to have worked altogether in favour of Ellaby's enemies."

"On the night of his disappearance," said Blake, "the woman, accompanied by a shabbily-dressed man, drove from Norfolk Street to Charing Cross Station, where she took two tickets for Paris. She and her companion both entered the Continental train, but it is quite certain they never went by it. They must have left it when it was on the point of starting."

"The booking to France was a mere blind—to lead you on a false scent. There can be no doubt that the woman is still in London, and probably not far off. Very likely the man who accompanied her was Dulk himself. Within a day or so someone will turn up at the London Joint Stock Bank with a cheque signed by the missing man. As we have warned the authorities at the bank to detain any such messenger, I hope to reach the conspirators through that means. There can be no doubt that their object is to extort money from their prisoner—"

"And when they have succeeded, what will become of him?" suggested Blake.

"Ah, that is just where all the danger comes is," said

126

Gervaise gravely.

"I wonder if the 'Red Lights' have any hand in the kidnapping?"

"Who and what are the 'Red Lights,' my friend?"

"It is a new and formidable society of professional lawbreakers of every class. Its conception was due to the fertile brain of a young, well-educated fellow named Leon Polti. It was his idea to join together into one powerful association the most expert operators in all branches of crime. The cleverest burglar throws in his lot with the most accomplished forger, and so on through the whole list of police offences. The notion is a brotherhood of crime, with meeting places, and correspondents all over the country, working for the common good of their own combination, and to the hurt of honest people. If Polti could realize his highest ideal and conduct such a gigantic organization, on strictly business principles, and with keen method, I fear the police would be beaten at every turn, and crime would be triumphant in the land! Luckily, rogues never do agree together for long.

"They will observe no laws—not even their own. So Politi's vast scheme will remain a dream, and nothing else, to the end of time. This case we have in hand looks something like the work of his gang. Watching and waiting for the rich man coming from Australia, and sending the woman over to Paris to shadow him suggests his methods. I daresay I can find him. He knows me. We will see if we can discover anything of his doings."

127

At this point their conversation was interrupted by the appearance of a shaggy, flaming head of red hair, which thrust itself into the office through the half-opened doorway.

"Well," interrogated Blake, "what do you want?"

"Please, governor, I'm the boy wot stands about the top of Essex Street, selling papers, and you've given me many a 'brown,' you has."

A body followed the head, and there stood disclosed to the two detectives, a short, bright-faced boy, who looked like nothing so much as an animated bundle of rages. His tattered trousers barely touched his knees, and strips of time-eaten cloth fluttered round his thin, discoloured arm.

"I've got no 'browns' for you to-day," said Blake, waving his hand impatiently.

"Oh yes, you has sir," the street boy answered, with a knowing shake of his glowing locks. "Wait till you 'ear wot I've to tell yer, and then I think you'll be good for a 'bob.' It's like this 'ere. Tommy Roundhead says as 'ow you want to find out about a 'toff' as was taken out of a house in Arundel Street, late Thursday night. Well, I can tell you all about that 'ere. 'Cos, why? I helped in the job myself."

"If you can help me to find that gentleman," said Blake, with sudden energy, "I'll make a man of you! We won't trouble about shillings. Pounds and pounds shall be spent on you."

"We can decide what to do when we have heard his tale," said Gervaise, with more caution.

"It's like this, governor. I was walking down Arundel Street, wondering where I should pitch myself for the night, when a four-wheeler drives up, and stops at that house. The driver jumps off the box, and I see, at once, that he weren't a reg'lar cabby. 'Ere young Vesuvius!' 'ee cries, "'old the 'osses 'ed.' The door of the 'house opens without him knocking or ringing. I sees that there's a sort of bed made up in the cab. In a minute or two the driver comes out with another man. Between them they carries a third man, who, if he ain't dead, 'as lost 'is senses. They puts this helpless chap inside, and the coachman springs on to his box again. 'I shall be there before you,' said the man who is standing on the pavement. He puts his 'and in 'is pocket, and after fumbling about a bit, he pull out 'arf a sovereign. 'Take that,' he says to me, 'I ain't got noffink smaller.' He walks away quick.

"'Well,' thinks I, 'if I gets 'arf a quid for 'olding the 'oss while they puts the swell into the cab, perhaps I shall get a bit more if I'm there to 'old it when they takes 'im *hout*.' So I gets up on the back of the cab, and clings on. But, bless you! I was taken right away to Barking. I didn't get off because I made sure the cab would be coming back again. At last we stops before a tumble-down old water-mill. Then the driver brings out a blunderbuss or somfink deadly, and a reg'lar hold-fashioned life preserver. I take to me 'eels in case they should want to give me one on the 'ed. I waits about hoping to see the cab go back. But they puts it in the stable there, and I 'as to walk. I fall in with a tramp, and he sneaks my half sovereign. Then the police collars me for being a wagabond, and that's how it is I ain't been at my hold pitch the last day or two."

"This is news indeed," exclaimed Gervaise. "Can you lead us to this old mill?"

"It's a hawful lonely place," said the boy, "but I think I can find it again."

"Let us go at once," suggested Gervaise.

"We must lose no time," agreed Blake, meditatively, "but we need to go to work with extreme caution. I don't like that remote water-mill. It looks murderous in my eyes. If our man is still there, and alive, his gaolers may offer a desperate resistance. The quickest way will be to take the train to Barking."

"Can't do it, governor," declared the lad; "I shall never find the place if I don't go the same way as that four-wheeler did."

So they hired a hansom, and it took half a day to light on the spot where "Bill Bender" had threatened Frank Ellaby with bludgeon and pistol.

"The place is deserted," said Blake. "I fear the worst."

"We shall have no difficulty in getting in," said Gervaise, as he threw the weight of his body against a rotten and ill-secured back door, which at once flew open.

The rats infesting the place scampered before them as they walked through the musty passages and gloomy rooms.

Upstairs they came on a heavy door, barred and bolted on the outside.

Their hearts beat high as they undid these fastenings.

They felt sure there were on the point of entering the room where Mr. Ellaby had been kept prisoner.

Would they find him there now, was the question which trembled on the lips of both, but neither spoke.

There were not hopeful of discovering him alive, for he had not answered the shouts they had raised on entering the building. Was his murdered body to meet their horrified gaze?

"Empty, as I suspected," said Gervaise. "What a strong room it is? It might have been built for a prison cell. He has been here, that is quite clear. There is his bed, his writing materials—"

"And" said Blake, "an absence of water and of other food!"

"They left him to starve to death!" Gervaise added excitedly, "but he has escaped by tearing the fire-grate from its settings. See how loose the bricks behind are. He could not have had great difficulty in making the hole through which he must have crawled. There is a room beyond—long, narrow. We must follow his example, and see where it leads to."

"His footprints on the dusty floor can still be traced," said Blake. "The open window at the end shows he escaped that way. Why has he not communicated with me?"

"Because," answered Gervaise impressively, "his body lies at the bottom of that still, black-looking pool. You observe,

131

this window is exactly over the old wheel of the water-mill. He must have stepped on to it. His weight would make it revolve; he would be hurled into the water. Probably one of the flanges would strike his head, and render him insensible. Then the weeds would catch him in their deadly embrace.

"See! There is his hat floating on the green scum! We must have this water dragged!"

As soon as they could procure drags and other aids, the pond was most effectually dragged.

After some hour's work, and with much difficulty, they brought a corpse to the bank, about which lank weeds still clung.

"Unhappily, we are too late to preserve the life of Frank Ellaby, for here his body undoubtedly lies. The one thing left for us is to make our very best effort to bring his murderers to justice."

It was Gervaise who spoke.

"And that we will do as certainly as we stand here," answered Sexton Blake.

CHAPTER V.

The Vicar's Secret—A True Lover—The Cheque
for £20,000—Arrested.

In this chapter we must take the reader to the old-fashioned Sussex village of Downslow, and to the ivy-clad rectory there, in the library of which sat the Rev. Frederick Briarton, in grave conversation with Ernest Truelove, a farmer's son, who was on the eve of leaving his old home for London, with the intention of entering one of its medical schools and winning a surgeon's diploma.

"I will not conceal from you my satisfaction at knowing that you have won the love of my dear Rose," said the

133

clergyman, "for I have confidence in your high regard for truth and honour. I am old, and it is idle for me to hope that I can be much longer in this world. I shall die the happier for knowing that Rose has linked her life with one who will do his utmost to shield her form its storms. But, my dear boy, I have a secret to confide to your keeping, which may make you desire to withdraw from the engagement you have entered into."

"Nothing can possible happen to make me do that," said Ernest, fervently.

"Prepare yourself for a shock my friend. *Rose is no daughter of mine!* I do not even know who her parents are."

"Yu have succeeded in surprising me," said young Truelove. "I love Rose for herself alone, and I care not whose child she is!"

"She is the essence of goodness and purity. Many years ago I was chaplain to one of Her Majesty's prisons. A few days before I resigned that appointment to commence duties at a small living in Yorkshire, which had been presented to me, one of the female convicts, a handsome and accomplished woman, sent for me, and upon her knees implored me to protect a little girl her arrest and sentence had compelled her to leave in the care of some rough, illiterate people living at Hammersmith. She said that the child was not her own, that it had a great future before it, and that when she was released she would repay me for my trouble, and restore the child to its proper sphere. As I had not been blessed with any children of my own, I was ready enough to adopt Rose. My poor dead wife grew devotedly attached to her, and she was brought up as our own daughter. The time soon came when I began to feel terror lest her convict guardian should appear at our home, and blight its happiness by claiming our darling Rose.

"By the will of an uncle I was practically compelled to change my old name of Sparrow to the one I now bear—Briarton. I have moved about a good deal, too, and perhaps that is why the woman has not found me. I am glad to have eluded her. It would go very much against my moral train to have to deliver up so pure and gentle a girl to a woman who has once worn a convict's dress. I have never had the courage to tell Rose the truth. She firmly believes herself to be my child."

"Let her die in that faith," said Truelove, promptly.

"It would be cruel to tell her the truth now, and no useful purpose would be served. She herself is too good for me to believe that her parents were bad. I will work hard, and in a little over three years I shall secure my diploma; then I can give her a name which shall be her very own, and she can defy anyone who may wish to claim her."

After this Ernest spent a long time with Rose herself, till the hour came when he had to drive to the station and catch his train. They had repeated their mutual vows over and over again.

When evening prayers were said in the vicarage, the rector introduced a fervent one for the safety and prosperity of Ernest Truelove, amid the pitfalls and temptations of the huge

135

metropolis.

Meanwhile this young gentleman, having spent an hour or so in Brighton, was dashing on to London at express speed, his regrets at leaving his old friends and the scenes of his youth lightened by his sense of the vivid change which was now to colour the daily routing of his life.

His only fellow-passenger was a young fellow who looked about his own age, but he might have been older. Slight in build, with a creamy skin, and large, dark, fascinating eyes, a round smooth chin, and a delicate mouth, he was decidedly effeminate in appearance, and yet there lurked in his very graceful movement a suspicion of sinewy and uncommon strength.

The two had easily fallen into conversation, and this had led to an exchange of cards.

The stranger's bore the name of—

"Leon Polti."

"So," said the latter, to whom the innocent Ernest had confided much of his past history and many of his plans for the future, "you want comfortable lodgings in the centre of London? Ah! Now I don't think you can do better than take up your quarters at the house where my sister and I are temporarily located—99, Bernard Street, Russell Square. It's no distance from Charing Cross Hospital. The landlady is the most obliging creature I ever met with, and the cooking is capital. I know she has a bed and sitting-room to let. Probably you don't mind if they are a bit high up. You can drive home with me to-night. There will be no harm in seeing the place, even if you should elect not to take the apartments."

"I am very much obliged to you," said Ernest. "I have no doubt the place will suit me very well indeed. I suppose, though, I shall have to go to a hotel to-night?"

"Not a bit of it! If you like the accommodation, Madame Dulk, the landlady, will make you perfectly comfortable at once."

Ernest was charmed with the house and with his new friends.

The same evening he dined with Mr. Polti, and he saw that this gentleman lived in quite high style. The table was spread with delicacies, in and out of season, and there were famous wines.

"My sister is out of town to-night," said his host. "I hope to introduce you to her to-morrow."

On the following morning he encountered a dark young lady on the stairs. The likeness to Leon Polti was so striking heat he could not doubt her near relationship to that gentleman, so he ventured to address her.

"Oh, yes," she said, with a laugh, which disclosed a set of brilliant teeth, "I am Nizza Polti. My brother has told me so much about you. I hope we shall be great friends. Some business has called him away; he will not be back for a few days. But," she added, "Madame Dulk generally sits with me in the evening,

137

and any time you like we shall be glad if you will join us."

The days passed very pleasantly with Ernest. Some evenings he saw Nizza, and on others Leon. Their own affairs so fell out that they were never able to be together when young Truelove was in the house.

One evening as Leon was sitting with the medical student in the latter's room, Madame Dulk tapped at the door, and brought word that a gentleman wanted below to see Mr. Polti on most urgent business.

"Bother him!" said Leon. "Can't he come in the morning?"

"No. he says it is imperative that you see him now."

"He shall wait till I have finished this cigar, at any rate. Tell him so, whoever he may be. I have these inquisitive people," he added, with a yawn, to Ernest.

When he did at last deign to descend the stairs he found Calder Dulk waiting for him. He took him into another room.

"You have an odd way of disturbing one at most inconvenient moments," said Leon. "Well, what is it you want me for?"

"The rat in his cage has eaten his cheese," replied Dulk, harshly, annoyed at the other's assumption of cool indifference. "In other words, Mr. Frank Ellaby has signed all the papers you made out for him to put his signature to. I've got them on me. It's for you to turn them into good current gold. Our part of the business is finished, and that has been the roughest and the worst

138

section of it. Now you can put in some of your 'fine' work, as you call it."

"I'm afraid you can come in a sneering mood, Dulk," Polti drawled his words out lazily. "And really it does not become so jovial a fellow as yourself. *What has been done with Ellaby?*"

"I left him to 'Bill Bender.' *You* know what he generally does with them."

"It's always force, and never persuasion, with you people," said Leon contemptuously.

"These papers seem to be all right," he continued. "They shall have my attention as soon as possible, and you will all know the result"

"That won't do for me," said Dulk fiercely. "I mean having the lion's share of this plunder. Why, if it hadn't been for me you would not have known of the existence of the Frank Ellaby. But for my wife's promptitude it might have taken you months to capture him. Those papers represent an actual little gold mine. It is through our work, and through the work of no one else, that they have been obtained, and we mean being paid in full! You talk about us all being equal. You are like the man in the play. He wanted his followers to be equal so long as he was chief. No doubt you would like to be crowned 'Monarch of Criminals,' and 'King of Crime,' and all that kind of thing; but we are not quite such fools as to give way to you."

"You amuse me, Dulk," said Leon, throwing himself

back in his chair, and smiling dangerously. "Perhaps you will condescend to remember that, but for me, there would have been no house in Arundel Street to take your victim to—the man you have twice plundered. But for me there would have been no old mill in which to torture him into subjection. But for me you would not now have good broadcloth on your back. But for me the only possible roof for you would be the strong one of the gaol. You want the lion's share of the money? You shall have it all, my friend. Take back your papers; do what you will with them. I wash my hands of the affair, of you, of your wife. You cannot play either the role of knave or honest man. Well, I am better without you. Good-night."

"Leon, Leon," pleaded Dulk, with a white, anxious face, "don't talk like that! You know I dare not work those papers! Come, come; forgive me! I spoke hastily; I did not mean what I said. Take the papers again. Work as you chose with them; I make no conditions."

"Make conditions!" repeated Leon. "The world must turn inside out before *you* will ever be able to dictate to *me*. Leave those documents. Go away. I will see what can be done. It is a risky business, and I know the hazard better than any of you. If a hitch occurs, there must be instant flight from here."

"Yes," said Polti to himself when he was alone; "I see that I am in the most danger from my own followers. They would kill me to gain possession of Frank Ellaby's money. Dulk is the most likely man to strike the first blow. Knowing where

140

my peril lies, I can evade it. Extreme caution and swift flight will save me, and nothing else. I thank thee, Fate, for throwing that innocent young Ernest Truelove in my way!"

On the following morning the student again met Nizza Polti on the stirs.

"My brother has been unexpectedly called away this morning before you were awake," she said in her pretty way, shedding the full light of her eyes on his face. "He wants you to do a small favour for him, and I am sure you will. It is only to get a cheque cashed at the London Joint Stock Bank, and meet him to-night at Charing Cross Railway Station with the money. He is going on to Paris with it."

"I shall be delighted to be of any service to him, and to you," said Ernest. "Why! this cheque is for £20,000! Quite a fabulous amount!"

"My brother's transactions often run into five figures," she answered, with a smile. "If the cheque were for a small sun, I could do the business myself. He prefers to trust it to you, because you are stronger and cleverer than I am."

"Directly I have had my breakfast I will go to the bank," declared Ernest, in his impulsive way.

"There is not such a great hurry. So long as you are at the bank by eleven o'clock, that will do."

Just as Ernest was leaving the house a cab drew up at the door. To his great surprise, it contained Rose and the Rev. Frederick Briarton.

It chanced that just as these two reached the house, Madame Dulk was standing at the dining room window, and she had a clear view of them.

She drew back hastily. Gleams of satisfaction shot from her eyes.

"At last I have found him!" she said to herself. "The clergyman to whom I confided the child. Doubtless that is Rose herself, grown into a beautiful woman. I will lose no time in regaining my prize. My husband and Polti and the rest may have their big hauls, but I shall now be better off than any of them."

"Dad had me come up to London by the very first train on some business in the City." Rose explained.

She was flushed with excitement, and with the delight she felt at seeing her lover again. "So I coaxed him to let me come, too."

"We thought we would give you a surprise," laughed the vicar," "and join you in a little lunch, if you have such a handy thing in the house."

"Only too delighted to see you," said Ernest; "but I must go to the City myself. We can all go together in the cab you have come by, and talk as we go.

"My business is with the Joint Stock Bank," he added, "and it won't occupy many minutes. After that I shall be entirely at your service. What do you think, Mr. Briarton? I'm going to change a cheque for twenty thousand pounds!"

The figures were sufficiently large to impress the rural

clergyman, and to awe Rose.

Ernest briefly explained how he chanced to be in possession of so valuable a piece of paper.

They watched him, as he, with a great air of importance (which he could not resist), entered the bank. They saw him emerge from its portals, and then a dreadful thing happened.

A tall, broad man tapped him on the shoulder.

Before he could say a word a pair of handcuffs were thrust on his wrists. Two other men came from across the road with a seeming air of authority. There were seized, too, and treated in the same way.

The police had taken Ernest Truelove into custody. They had also arrested Mr. Gervaise, of Pairs, and Mr. Sexton Blake, very much to the complete dismay of both these notable detectives.

Calder Dulk and Leon Polti watched these proceedings from a safe corner, and then made off with all speed possible.

Poor Rose uttered a cry of distress, and the Reverend Mr. Briarton sprang onto the pavement and was at once in the midst of the excited group, standing shoulder to shoulder with Mr. Frank Ellaby!

CHAPTER VI.

The Release of the Prisoners—Flying from Justice—"I will Kill You Both."

"So I have made a good haul and caught you all at once," said Ellaby, with a grim smile. "I am sorry you have turned out a rogue, Gervaise, for I had formed another opinion of you. I did hope that you, Sexton Blake, were honest, yet you have joined in as vile a conspiracy against my life and fortune as man could devise. As for you," he added, addressing Ernest Truelove, "you have a noble, manly face, which makes me sorry to see you associated with these rascals."

"I do not know what all this means," declared the Rev.

144

Frederick Briarton, "but I do aver that this young gentleman never did a dishonourable action in his life, and if you dare to detain him, it will be at your own peril. He was simply asked to get this cheque cashed by people who lodge in the house where he has apartments."

"It was Leon Polti's sister," Ernest commenced.

"Ah!" Blake interrupted, "this, as I guessed, is the work of the 'Red Lights,' and I hope we shall be able to capture and convict the whole gang. I forgive you, Mr. Ellaby, for thinking I had something to do with your kidnapping; but had you gone to Scotland Yard, instead of to the City Police, you would have heard that Gervaise and myself have toiled day and night to rescue you. Only yesterday we discovered the old mill. We had the pond dragged, and we found one body, which, at first, we thought was yours—"

"No, I am still alive," said Frank, "though I did get a ducking there. I hope, Blake, your tale is true."

"If we all drive to Scotland Yard, you will soon be satisfied on that point. It's my opinion, Mr. Ellaby, that this young man has simply been the dupe for the daring Polti crowd."

"I am a clergyman of the Church of England," said Mr. Briarton; "and I have known Ernest Truelove for many years. I am convinced he is incapable of committing a criminal action. I must insist on his immediate release from custody."

"Oh, Rose, Rose!" said Ernest, as his *fiancée* joined the throng. "I do wish you have been spared the pain of seeing me so disgraced."

"So your name is Rose?" questioned Frank Ellaby, regarding her fair, fresh young face with interest. "Many years ago I had a little girl stolen from me bearing that name. She must be about your age now. I would give much to find her."

"That is a matter we can discuss some other time," declared the rector, and with such significance that a sudden hope sprung up in Frank's heart. "Ernest Truelove must be released!"

It took very little time to prove how far from the truth was the charge against Messrs. Sexton Blake and Gervaise, to whom Mr. Ellaby made a most handsome apology.

Nor was it long before this gentleman was persuaded to withdraw every imputation against Ernest Truelove; and later, when he knew more of him, he decided to make him reparation for the wrong to which he had been subjected.

They all journeyed to Bernard Street, hoping to effect the capture of madame Dulk and Nizza Polti, if not of Polti himself.

No one answered their repeated knocks of continuous ringing of the bell.

"The birds have flown," said Blake. "No doubt Mr. Truelove was shadowed to the bank. When he was seen to be taken into custody the warning note was sounded, and the ducks have taken unto themselves wings and vanished. Gervaise and I will see that the railway stations and the wharves are watched. Every effort shall be made to prevent the escape of the culprits.

146

Now we know them there should not be any difficulty about this. You gentlemen had best make yourselves comfortable at some good family hotel where I can visit you later on, and report progress. Say the Silver Bell, at Charing Cross. I really don't think you can help us now in any way. Too many cooks, you know, spoil even a good broth."

"All my personal belongs are in that house," said Ernest, ruefully looking up at its windows.

"I daresay you will get your luggage all right," returned Gervaise, with a smile, "but that is a department of our business which can afford to wait. We have not a moment to lose, so farewell, my friends!"

Gervaise was right. Every second was precious. Already much valuable time had been squandered.

Even as he spoke, Calder Dulk and Nizza Polti stood on the platform of King's Cross Station ready to step into a fast train soon to start for one of the Northern centres.

The appearance of Mr. Frank Ellaby outside the bank had filled Dulk with the direst consternation. He judged there could be no safety for him in England now, especially as Ernest was in custody, and could put them on the track of Madame Dulk, who had gone he knew not where.

"Ah!" he said, when he and Nizza had settled themselves in the carriage, and the train was almost on the move, "we shall get out of London all right, and then entire escape won't be so very difficult."

The whistle sounded, and the great engine gave one mighty gasp of relief.

There were on the move, when the door was torn open, and a man threw himself into the carriage.

"Keep still," he yelled, placing himself opposite them. "If you move an inch I'll shoot you both like the dogs you are."

He pointed a pistol at each head.

"So," he continued, "you've got possession of my share—me, who has done all the work, too! It isn't the first time you have tried on that game; but it shall be the last. You look very pretty in that woman's disguise, Leon Polti; but it won't work with me, because I know it. I always swore if a pal played me false that I would kill him. *I mean to kill you both!*"

They knew that their first stoppage was Peterborough, and that they were completely at the mercy of this desperate man, who was none other than Bill Bender, and who laughed to scorn the terrors of the law.

CHAPTER VII.

A Struggle for Life—Thrown from the Train.

It was some time before the two men recovered from their surprise.

"Don't be a fool, Bill Bender. We have not got a farthing of Frank Ellaby's money. The game is up; the detectives are after the lot of us. We are flying out of London, and mean to lie quiet in the country for a time; that's why we are in this train."

It was Calder Dulk who spoke, half pleadingly, and with somewhat of a reassuring tone to Bill Bender, who still covered him and Nizza Polti with his pistols.

Dulk looked very helpless with the muzzle of the deadly weapon pointed straight at his heart.

149

"You always were an idiot, Bender," said Nizza, talking in his natural voice—for Nizza and Leon were one.

The disguise was so perfect that only very few of his own followers knew that he did not possess a sister.

By the aid of this change of costume he had more than once deceived his confederates, and passed freely out from among them, when very little would have made them tear him to pieces.

"Put those silly things down. They are more likely to hurt you than me."

"I am glad you have turned up," Leon added in his cool, business way. "I wanted to see you. I fancy we may yet get hold of that money, and want your help, my friend Bender."

They had emerged from King's Cross tunnel now, and were beginning to whiz along at a rate which soon promised exciting speed.

"None of that for me," said Bill. "I've had lots of it from you, and I know you. Now then, young gentleman in the skirts, tumble up the gold. You had the cheque right enough, and you've got the money."

"Certainly I had the cheque," acknowledged Leon quietly, "but you don't suppose I was going to be so foolish as to present it myself?"

"No," growled Bill, "you've been clever enough to leave me to be the only one who can be identified as being connected with this job. One wears a mask and the other hides himself.

Then you try to do me out of the money and leave me to swing, while you enjoy yourselves with wine and other luxuries."

"I sent a young country friend of mine to the bank to get Frank Ellaby's cheque cashed," Leon spoke impressively, "and I suppose he got the money. Dulk and I watched him from a safe distance to see if things were all right. All we know is, that when our young friend left the bank he was taken in charge by the police. Just pay particular attention to this, Bill—*Frank Ellaby was there, too, waiting for him!*"

"What!" exclaimed Bill, so astonished at the news that he relaxed a trifle of his vigilance.

"How could he have escaped from the mill? I made sure he was a corpse by this time. He won't rest till he finds me. Yah!" he exclaimed, with a sudden change of demeanor, "you think I am a kid, and you are trying to put me off with these fairy tales till we stop somewhere, where you think you can get help. Come on, pay up, or I'll fire."

"Don't be so thick-headed, Bill; I tell you we have not got the money. Besides, I should never think of swindling *you*; you are far too useful to us. Why don't you search us? Perhaps that will satisfy you. You can commence with me."

"So I will," said the thoughtless ruffian, laying his pistols by his side.

Leon was full of tricks. This proposal was only a ruse to put Bill Bender off his guard, and to enable them to deprive him of his weapons.

It would have succeeded admirably had not Leon been too quick.

He stretched his white hand over to secure the deadly weapons before Bill had half risen from his seat.

The burly bully saw what was intended, and Leon was felled to the floor of the carriage, rendered insensible, and his body kicked under a seat in less time than it takes to write these lines.

Thinking *his* opportunity had come, Calder Dulk now sprung on Bill Bender, to be received by him in his powerful grip.

Dulk was a man of weight and muscle.

Knowing the one he had to deal with, he was sure this might prove a struggle for very life.

Nothing would ever now persuade Bill that there had been no intention to deprive him of his share in the cheque obtained by such desperate means. His teeth were set. His eyes stood out of his head. His whole system throbbed with one idea, and it was a fierce one—to crush Dulk.

This so absorbed his every faculty that he did not hear the rush through the air of the train, the rattle of the carriages, or the frequent wild shrieks of the engine.

No pleadings for mercy from human tongue could touch him!

Dulk's veins rose upon his forehead, knotted and black. His face was horror-stricken. He knew that a relentless demon

152

was grappling with him, and it could only be by a superhuman effort that he could escape the death sentence written on that implacable face.

Strive his utmost he did, straining every muscle and nerve.

At one moment the two stood silent, and looking as firm as a pair of Roman wrestlers cut in marble. When the train gave a lurch they were thrown heavily with it. Then came a fierce , panting struggle on the floor. Some seconds one had the advantage, to be quickly wrenched from him by the other.

As they managed at last to struggle to their feet, they never for an instant released their hold on each other.

A thick hot breath fanned their cheeks as a blast from a furnace all the time. The solid seating on each side of them in the narrow passage of that compartment made it difficult for either to throw the other.

So each strove with slow, persistent effort to reach the pulsating throat of the other.

Bill Bender was the first to win in this deadly effort.

As his thumb and finger closed on Calder Dulk's throat, a groan of triumph escaped him. Now he could throw his whole weight against his victim, for with the latter's lack of breath the muscles of his arms and legs relaxed.

The two fell against the carriage door. A third of Dulk's body was already out of the open window, which had no protecting rail in the middle of it.

Just then they were entering a tunnel.

"You are best out altogether!" growled Bill, lifting up the legs of the man, and letting him drop out into the darkness.

A crimson flash of light from the fire of the engine illuminated his ghastly white face as he was swallowed up by the relentless black of the stifling excavation.

"It's Leon Polti who has the money; that's certain, or he would not be got up like a girl," muttered Bill, and he at once commenced to roughly search that gentleman.

"The other has got it after all!" he cried, in disgust. "There all that money lies on the line for any navvy or porter, or anyone to have for the finding. I *must* have a try for it."

The signal towards the exit of the tunnel was against the train, and it slowed.

Bill took advantage of this opportunity, and he dropped gently off the footboard into the gloom.

Leon, now he was alone, sprang to his feet, and, taking down a small bag from the luggage-rail, he quickly made a complete transformation in his dress.

When the train stopped at Peterborough, and he stepped gingerly from his carriage, he appeared in such attire as would have befitted the most exacting up-to-date Bond Street swell.

"I am glad Bill and Dulk have both gone that way," he reflected, with an amiable smile. "It is an experience they are not likely to recover from, and they were beginning to get troublesome."

154

CHAPTER VIII.

The Drugged Coffee—Coronet or Grave?

While the detectives were pursuing their investigations, Frank Ellaby's party engaged quarters at that cosy and eminently respectable hostelry, the Silver Bell.

Here it naturally followed that Ernest should seek the companionship of Rose, and that Mr. Briarton and Frank Ellaby should exchange confidences one with another.

"From what you have told me," said the latter, "I have little doubt, in my own mind, that your Rose and the little girl my dying sister entrusted to my care are one and the same.

"The woman from whom you received her said no idle

155

words when she declared that the child had a great future before her, for I can give her much wealth.

"Though I never liked Calder Dulk's wife, I did not regard her as a criminal, though, seeing that she robbed me, the news need not surprise me. Odd, indeed it is that I should once more be thrown into her clutches.

"Someone has truly said that we all live our lives twice over. Certainly, our experiences have a way of repeating themselves in the strangest manner.

"I quite agree with you, that it would be unwise to say anything to the young lady at present touching her real identity, which I fear we shall never discover, unless we can force that woman Dulk to give up the papers she stole from my sister's escritoire.

"If we once catch her, a promise to withdraw my prosecution against her may work wonders."

"I trust that she and her evil companions may soon be brought to justice," said the clergyman. "They might have ruined my friend, Ernest Truelove, who is so honest himself that he suspects no one. I will remain in London a few days, and see how the search progresses."

"Dad," cried rose, entering the apartment at that moment, "there is to be a splendid concert at St. James's Hall tonight. Do, please, let us go."

"Certainly. We will all go," laughed Frank. "I will send round to the box-office and secure seats at once. Should Blake want us, we can leave word where we are to be found."

The concert-room was crowded, and on leaving it they became involved in the whirl of a fashionable crush.

Frank Ellaby had called for a cab. While they waited for it a rush from behind separated Rose from her friends.

"This way, miss," said a man to her; "the cab is waiting for you."

She followed the fellow in all simplicity, and soon she was sitting inside a soft, delicately-perfumed vehicle, which drove off at a furious rate before she realized what she had done.

A lady, beautifully dressed, sat facing her.

She smiled kindly on the young and agitated girl.

"There is some mistake. I have lost my friends. Oh, pray forgive me for getting into your carriage instead of our cab. Please tell your coachman to stop," cried Rose in alarm.

"I saw your mistake and it amused me," said the lady. "I dearly love a little joke. Tell me where you wish to go to and my man shall drive us there."

"But my friends—" Rose commenced.

"You will be home before them, and will have the laugh against them. That is all. They deserve a taste of anxiety for losing you. The Silver Bell Hotel? I know it quite well. My house lies the same way, but it comes first.

"We will pause there for a moment, if you don't mind, and then I will take you to your own people."

The splendour of the equipage in which she found

herself and the aristocratic bearing of the white-haired lady, who patronized her with such an easy grace, were sufficient to lull all suspicion of foul play in Rose's mind.

"Indeed, she felt that she was an intruder there, and she considered her hostess very gracious in treating her with such good humour.

They pulled up outside a large but dismal-looking house.

"Here we are at my home," said the lady. "Come in with me, if only for a minute. Nay, I insist. You are too nervous to be left alone. Come! We shall yet reach the Silver Bell before your folks get there."

The door of the building opened, and without hands it seemed. Silently it closed behind them, leaving them in a dark passage.

"Take my hand," said her conductress in a more commanding voice.

"I will lead you to the light!"

Rose began to feel frightened now, but she had no choice but to follow her guide along the black corridor, down a number of steps, then to the sill open air, again into another building, and up a high flight of stairs.

"Open for us Belus—open!" said the woman.

Rose was now conscious that some creature was walking in front of them.

She could hear its breath coming and going quickly, but its footfall made no sound, and she wondered whether it was a monkey or a human being.

Suddenly her eyes were blinded by a great flood of light.

She stood in one of the most lavishly-furnished rooms her imagination could conceive.

She saw that "Belus" was a dreadfully attenuated man. His skin was dry and yellow, and his flesh all withered up like that of a mummy, to which he bore a strong resemblance.

The horribleness of his appearance was increased by the fact that he had lost one eye, and one arm was gone.

These injuries were all on his left side, and they suggested that he had at some period of his existence been involved in a terrible accident.

"Belus has been with me for many years," said the strange lady, "and he is very faithful."

"Unto death," declared the ghastly-looking Belus.

"It is well said," laughed his mistress. "Unto death! Get us coffee," she added.

"Indeed, indeed," protested Rose. "I must not stay. Do, please, let me go to my friends. They will be quite upset at my disappearance."

"We will leave here within ten minutes," said the lady, smilingly. "The coffee will revive you. I shall feel hurt if you do not take it."

It proved to be a delicious decoction of the glorious Arabian berry, and it was served in tiny gold cups chased in a most elegant way; but it had not the effect of stimulating Rose.

159

On the contrary, it made her so drowsy that in a couple of minutes she was sound asleep on the luxurious sofa on which she had been induced to sit!

Her hostess stood over her, and regarded her prostrate figure with an expression of evil triumph.

"What is this?" asked Belus, creeping to her side, "revenge or merely simple villainy?"

"Greed," answered the woman shortly. "This girl is worth much money to me.

"Hark! That is the duke's knock. Take care he does not enter here. Nor must he know of this girl's presence in this house. The time is not yet ripe for the disclosure I have to make. Go to him. You may tell him that I am here, and would see him on a matter of grave importance.

"Do my bidding well, my faithful Belus, and I will reward thee."

"Yes," muttered the man, as he seemed to melt from the room, "as you did before, with the loss of an arm and an eye. Your rewards are perfect, and so shall be my revenge!"

"Ah! my beautiful Rose," reflected the woman, unable to take her eyes off her prisoner.

"What is to be your fate? Are you destined for an early grave, or will you soon wear one of England's noblest coronets?"

CHAPTER IX

One Thousand Pounds Reward—The Duke
of Fenton—A Sudden Death.

"Where is Rose," demanded Ernest, as the three men clustered round the cab.

"She was by my side a second ago," said Frank Ellaby.

"It is but this moment that I spoke to her," declared Mr. Briarton. "It is ridiculous to suppose she has lost us."

They looked in every direction. They waited till the crush had spent itself, and the pavement was pretty clear, and to their confusion they could see nothing of her.

They returned to the hall; she was not there.

161

The neighborhood was searched, police and cabmen question, and they could gain no tiding of the missing lady.

The extraordinary mystery of her disappearance appalled them. It was as though she had been suddenly swept off the face of the earth.

They made haste back to the hotel, hoping against hope, that, by some possibility, she might have reached it first. Only disappointment awaited them.

The clergyman and Ernest Truelove were both plunged into the deepest distress and consternation.

Frank Ellaby, too, was greatly concerned. It seemed absurd that he should no sooner find the girl he had been searching for all these years than he should allow her to be snatched from him again.

"It is past all comprehension," he said, "that with three of us to guard her, she should be taken from us in this miraculous way. It makes one believe in the supernatural. If money will bring her back she will soon be with us again. I will offer a thousand pounds reward for her recovery. The advertisements shall be sent to-night to all the daily papers."

"I think you heartily for that generous decision," said Ernest, "but we must strain every nerve to find her ourselves."

"And pray fervently to the One above to bless and protect her," said Mr. Briarton.

Before the missives to the newspapers could be dispatched, Sexton Blake called on them to report such progress as he had made in the hunting down of the "Red Lights."

The discovery of the body of a murdered man in the pool by the old mill had made this a police business.

Mr. Blake's efforts were confined solely to the interests of Frank Ellaby, who had now greater reason than ever for desiring to secure Calder Dulk and his desperate wife.

The detective listened to the story of Rose's disappearance with some surprise.

"I can only suppose," he said "that this is the work of the daring woman who stole the young lady before. How she managed to accomplish her purpose so easily, and in the full blaze of Piccadilly, I do not know.

"Doubtless her object is extortion. She is determined not to let you escape her, Mr. Ellaby. If the young lady is in her poser, I can promise you that I will soon bring about her release. Now that I know this woman Dulk, it will not be long before I find her."

"They are an exceedingly slippery gang to deal with. For instance, I have absolute proof that Calder Dulk and Nizza Polti left King's Cross this morning by the North express, which makes its first stoppage at Peterborough.

"I wired to that old cathedral city to have these two people detained until I arrived there, and formally charged them. No one answering their descriptions was to be found in the whole train!

"Indeed, it chanced, that there was only one lady 'on

board', and she is the daughter of a well-known clergyman.

"The train goes at a break-neck speed all the way, the guard is certain that no one left it *en route*, and that Nizza Polti and her male companion were in their carriage when it started from King's Cross.

"They have managed to do the vanishing trick to perfection."

"If that gang have succeeded in capturing poor Rose, they hold a trump card. I shall not dare to proceed against them for fear of imperiling her life. They are quite capable of using her as a shield to protect them from my vengeance."

It was Ellaby who spoke.

"That is true," Blake allowed ruefully. "But if they escape your active hostility, they have still to reckon with the police.

"The offer of a thousand pounds reward will bring a communication from some of them, I'm sure."

While this conversation was taking place in the Silver Bell Hotel, another, and ever more important one, was being carried on in the strange house whither Rose had been so cleverly conveyed.

Madame Dulk had left her beautiful and unconscious prisoner still reclining on the luxurious couch.

Entering another apartment, more superbly furnished than the first, madame found a tall, stoutly-built, aristocratic gentleman waiting for her.

He had keen, grey eyes, which glittered under his grey, heavy eyebrows. His white hair was clipped short to his military-looking head, and his moustache was well trimmed and intensely black.

"I received you message," he said in cold haughty tone, "and I have come. What have you to tell me now?"

"Will your Grace not deign to take a seat?" said Madame, humbly. "The missing child is again found. Of course she has grown to be a woman now. She is beautiful, and would ornament the highest station in the land."

"Tut!" he spoke impatiently; "what an old story this is! Woman, if you are in difficulties and want money, why not tell me so, and take your chance whether I give it to you or not? Why do you always try to touch my purse by some untruthful story?"

"Never, your Grace, never in my life!" protested Madame. "I have been mistaken before—that is all. I have never willfully deceived you. This time I have made no error. I have seen the minister who took possession of her when I was in prison. She is with him now.

"But the danger which threatens you is to be found in the fact that the brother of the woman who had her as a baby in Australia is here, and with her. He came over expressively to find her, and to vindicate her rights.

"He is enormously rich, and he will spend all he is worth in striving to establish her true identity. With my assistance he might learn this in half-an-hour.

"Now it is for your Grace's consideration whether you will submit to be compelled by law to accept this young lady as the daughter of your late elder brother, and allow her to take over the estates you now possess.

"You can arrange matters with me so that the proof of Lady Rose Fenton's existence can be forever destroyed, and she herself be removed to some safe place abroad.

"As she has never known the joys for the position she is legally entitled to, she can never miss them."

The Duke of Fenton, resting his head on his hand, sat for some minutes without speaking.

"It is a hard problem to solve," he muttered. "If I had only myself to consider, this girl might take her place in our family without hindrance from me. I doubt whether it would be good for her. One has to be bred up to a coronet to war it with ease.

"But my son, my dear and only son! The sudden appearance of this cousin of his would play sad havoc with his financial position!

"What do you propose, Madame?" he added in a louder tone, and looking up sharply at her.

"I propose that you should have a few days to prosecute your own inquiries about the Rev. Briarton and his so-called daughter," was the woman's prompt reply.

"While you are thus engaged, I undertake to get

possession of the young lady, and have her snugly housed at the big place in Bedfordshire.

"Then I will hand her over to you with all the proofs as to her birth parentage, and so on.

"Then it will be for you to decide what to do with her. You are already satisfied that such a lady does exist."

"Your terms?" he repeated, waving his hand impatiently.

"Two thousand pounds!"

"Set about your business," he said. And as he rose he allowed a deep sigh to escape him.

"Remember, not a hair of her head must be injured; not a cruel word must be said to her.

"Do not forget that the blood of the Fentons flows in her veins. Woe betide you if you do not pay it proper respect!"

He strode from the room, and out of the house, with a grand, haughty air.

At his carriage door his valet waited for him. The man had made such haste to be there that he was out of breath.

The few words he did utter were sufficient to send the proud nobleman reeling into his equipage as though he had been stabbed to the heart.

"What can have happened?" asked Madame, nervously.

She had followed "his Grace" to the door.

"His son is dead," said Belus, who was by her side. "His only son has been struck down suddenly in the billiard room of his club; heart disease, they say.

167

"So much for the pride of birth and the joy of riches! These aristocrats despise us and trample on us, but they all have to die—oh, yes, they all have to die!"

CHAPTER X.

Rose Awakes—A Long Ride—The Country House—Leon Polti's New Plot.

When Rose did at last recover her senses her brain was dizzy and numbed, and her muscles felt sore, as though she had been bruised. Heavy curtains were drawn across the windows, and lights were still burning, so she did not know whether it was night or morning.

She felt as though she had been unconscious for a long, long time. Her recollection returned slowly, and in a blurred, indistinct form.

"Thank goodness, you are once more in possession or

your faculties," said Madame, who was sitting by her side. She spoke with great fervor.

"Your papa has only just gone away. Do you know you have lain there like one in a trance for two days?

"The doctor says it is one of the most singular cases he has met with in the whole of his professional experience. He fancies that a small clot of blood must have gone into one of the minute blood–vessels of the brain, and pressing on that important organ, rendered you insensible.

"He advised us that directly consciousness returned to you all danger was passed, and that you would be your old self again, as by a miracle. So you must rise now, and take some sustenance.

"Then I will convey you to a pretty place in the country, which your friends have taken for you, and where they are waiting for you."

The poor girl, still suffering from the effects of the powerful drug which had been administered to her, listened to these words in hopeless bewilderment.

Judging from her own feelings, had she been told that she had lain there a week, she would have believed the tale. At any rate, she could do nothing now but obey her hostess. What little strength she had was swallowed up in wonder.

An appetizing meal was put before her. She partook sparingly of it, yet it revived her. She was soon ready, and anxious to leave that place, hoping most devoutly that she was really to be taken to her father—or rather to the good old man she had all these years regarded as being her parent.

Bur for the fact that as she passed out of the front door she saw a patch of blue sky above her, walking into the vehicle which was waiting was like stepping from one room into another.

The fact was, a large "pantechnicon" had been backed up close to the entrance to the house, and its folding doors at its end being opened, made a closed-in passage from the hall of the dwelling to the interior of the van.

So no strange, curious eyes could see Rose leave that residence, and all view of the street she was in was shut out from her.

A swing lamp hanging from the roof diffused a pleasant light through the interior. The floor was heavily carpeted.

There was a comfortable sofa, some easy chairs; a good solid table stood towards the far end, and handy to it were lockers containing crystal, cutlery, wines, and food.

An oil-stove made cooking possible, and a speaking tube rendered instructions to the driver easy.

It was certainly the warmest way of traveling by road that could well be devised.

There were many conspicuous evidences to prove that Rose was not its first passenger. When Madame and her prisoner had once entered the van, the man, who was to drive them, closed the doors sharply, and barred them.

The horses started off at a sharp trot.

"Now, my dear," said Madame, decisively, "make yourself comfortable, and don't attempt any fuss, or bother me with stupid questions. You are with friends, and that is quite enough for you to know. Later you shall be told all the fine things that are in store for you!"

"But," faltered poor Rose, "am I not to be taken to my father?"

"Why, of course you are! Have I not told you so? There now, amuse yourself with some of these books while I read the paper."

It was, perhaps, as well for Rose that she was too dazed just then to feel any particular alarm. It all felt like a dream, and not an entirely unpleasant one.

She attempted to read, but drowsiness assailed her, and she continued to drop into short, fitful sleeps, which seemed to tire her more than refresh her

They had a comfortable lunch, for which she had but small desire, and then came a cup of tea, which failed to refresh her.

On, still they went, keeping up a round pace all the time. They had four good horses, and Rose fancied that these were changed at least once during one of their many short stoppages.

It must have been towards evening when Madame herself dropped into a doze. The atmosphere of that van was close, and conducive to sleep.

172

Rose languidly picked the newspaper off this lady's lap.

For some reason, which she herself cold not have explained, she was rejoiced to see that its date was the one following the night she visited St. James's Hall.

So she had *not* been unconscious for two days, as she had been told.

Then her eyes caught sight of the advertisement, offering one thousand pounds reward for her safe recovery.

Her friends were on the alert, and she felt sure that she would soon be free.

She did not think it possible that in law-abiding England anyone could be long detained against his will, except in a prison or a lunatic asylum.

For her own safety's sake, she determined to take things quite calmly, to show no excitement, and to obey any reasonable command she might receive.

It would require an effort to hide her anxiety, and some courage to affect cheerfulness, when she was all terror in her uncertainty as to what designs her captors had on her.

She felt strong and brave enough to play the difficult part she had set before herself, and by enacting it well she hoped to soon effect her own escape, even if Mr. Briarton failed to find her.

The moon showered its light on them, and the stars twinkled with a frosty brightness when they at last drew up before a large, old-fashioned, substantial country house, which

173

stood in the midst of thickly-timbered grounds.

The hall door was open, and in the yellow glow of the gas was seen the form of Leon Polti.

"You here?" cried Madame, in a tone of distinct anger. "Why have you come to this place?"

"I expect for the same reason as yourself!" he answered, lightly. "For safety. Everything has failed—all has gone wrong. We are all scattered like chaff before the four winds!"

"Enough!" said the woman, curtly. "You and I will discuss business matters later. This way, my dear Rose. You will find you r room has been made very comfortable for you."

"I wonder who her pretty friend is?" muttered Leon, as he threw himself on a sofa before a bright fire in one of the sitting-rooms.

"The conditions of our confederation compel me to make you welcome, Leon Polti, anywhere and at any time. But I am sorry you are here to-night. I wish you had not come.

"Besides, I have done with the 'Red Lights' forever! Some of you are clever enough men, and you do great things when you work alone. When together, all you seem to do is to get in each other's way.

"I, at any rate, can afford to do without you."

This was what Madame said when she rejoined him.

"Ah," said Leon, with a cynical smile. "You have thought so before to-night. I have some news for you—your husband is dead!"

"Dead?" she echoed, starting to her feet. Then she fell back in her chair, and again repeated the dread words, "Calder Dulk is dead!"

"Well, I saw Bill Bender throw him out of a quick-going train on to the rails and in a tunnel. He seemed half dead before he left us. I don't think he can possibly be alive."

"You saw this, and raised no hand to protect him?"

"I was almost insensible myself. It's a miracle I escaped the same fate. Bender believes that we played him false. He'll do his best to kill me if he ever catches me. As for being here, I won't trouble you for long. All I want is to hide for a few days. By the way, who is your young friend?"

"That, Leon Polti, is my own particular business. She is worth more to me than all your abortive schemes put together would have been, even had you brought them to a successful issue. And I share with no one!"

"Don't you," Leon muttered, after madame had left him to his own reflections.

"Let me look at that advertisement again. 'One thousand pounds reward.' Ah! A nice little sum.

"Yes, as far as I can judge, the description of the missing lady tallies with that of the one who has just arrived. What an odd thing they don't give her name. Some reason for it, I suppose. 'Clothes marked, R.B.—Apply Proprietor, Silver Bell Hotel.'

"It would be rather amusing were I to snatch this

175

pleasant little prize from your grasp, Madame Dulk? I want a thousand pounds quite as much as you do.

"Nothing can be done till the morning, when I will contrive to get a look at the stolen beauty."

CHAPTER XI.

Sexton Blake has news—The Last of Calder Dulk—A Duke's
Repentance—Baffled by Suicide—A Message from Rose.

A few days had passed, and to the surprise of Sexton
Blake no one had yet made any serious application for the
thousand pounds reward so widely advertised.

Suggestions, descriptions, and offers of help they had
from all parts of the country, but nothing that promised the quick
return of Rose.

As Mr. Briarton and Frank Ellaby were discussing one of
their gloomy breakfasts, Mr. Sexton Blake entered the coffee-
room, and took a chair at their table.

177

"I have some news," he said disconsolately. "I have found Calder Dulk."

"Good!" cried Frank, "through him we may get Rose, if his wife has had anything to do with the dear girl's disappearance."

"I fear he is past giving help to us, or to anyone. Someone has been before you with his vengeance. Dulk is dead!"

"How did it come about?" asked Ellaby, in a low tone.

"His body was found in a tunnel, on the Great Northern Railway. It must have dropped from the North express I told you he and Nizza Politi took tickets by.

"He might have fallen out by accident, or he might have committed suicide; but both these theories are negatived by the fact that his throat, even yet, bears the impress of a powerful thumb and finger, which must have exercised sufficient pressure there to throttle him."

"Surely Nizza Polti had not enough strength—"

"Dear me, no. Indeed, it seems pretty clear that there never was any sister, and that is how I and Scotland Yard have been so often tricked on to wrong scents. Leon and Nizza are one.

"I managed at Peterborough to get permission to examine all the luggage that had come by that particular train, and which had been left in the cloak room.

"This chanced to consist of one petite portmanteau. It

contained a regularly built-up woman's costume, such as are used by female impersonators on the stage, only more delicately manufactured, to suit a drawing-room. The wig was a work of art. *Now* I understand why no Nizza could be found in that train. Leon had entered it a King's Cross as a girl, and had left it at Peterborough in his proper male attire.

"It turns out, too, that a man answering the description of the fellow who left you to starve at the water-mill, jumped into the carriage in which Polti and Dulk were, just as the train was on the move.

"Bill Bender, they call him. There is not a worse ruffian unhanged. I suppose he and Dulk quarreled—quarrelling is the one great characteristic of the criminal character—and Bill Bender strangled him, and then threw him on the line.

"So far the murderer has made good his escape. But the police are keen after him all over the country, and after the whole gang.

"I think we shall see a quick extinction of the 'Red Lights of London.'"

Ernest Truelove just then returned from an early lecture at his college. Truth to tell, his mind was too much stirred with anxiety for the safety of Rose to benefit from the learning which had been poured into it.

"I suppose you have no news of Miss Briarton?"

His tone was one of reproach and hopelessness.

The grief which he could never escape from had made its

179

impress on his face.

"You are wrong," Mr. Truelove, this time," said the detective, with a faint smile. "I bring you great news. No less personage than the Duke of Fenton himself shall restore Miss Rose Briarton to you. Perhaps, my dear sir, you will read that letter, and loud."

He handed envelope to the astonished clergyman, who opened it and repeated its contents, which ran as follows:—

"Rev. and Dear Sir,—

"We, as solicitors to the duke of Fenton, are instructed by his Grace to ease your anxiety as to the welfare of the young lady to whom you have so kindly acted as guardian for some years past.

"He believes that it is within his power to being about her return to you with little or no delay.

"With this view he desires that you meet him at our offices to-day at 12 o'clock, when he trusts to be in a position to discuss with you this young lady's real position in society, and her prospects, with more freedom than is consistent with such a purely professional communication as this.

"We are, Rev. and Dear Sir,

"Your obedient Servants,

"Martindale & Co."

"What does this mean?" Mr. Briarton, wonderingly, "and what can the duke of Fenton have to do with my Rose?"

"Simply and briefly," said Sexton Blake, "the facts seem

to be these. Martindale and I were schoolboys together at Winchester, and knowing I had this matter in hand, he confided the true state of affairs to me last night.

"It is clear that the late Duke of Fenton (the present Duke's elder brother), was a somewhat adventuresome young man, and that during his travels in Australia he fell in love with, and married, a lady who had everything to recommend her except birth and fortune.

"He persuaded her to keep the union a secret until he had at least seen his parents, and had endeavoured to win their countenance to this wedding of wealth with poverty. The ship he sailed in from Melbourne unhappily sank, and he, with many others, was drowned.

"His wife lodged with your sister, Mr. Ellaby, and in her house she died suddenly, before she could know her husband's sad fate.

"I need not tell you how Miss Ellaby left the child to your care, or how the papers establishing her right to the title of Lady Fenton excited the cupidity of the Dulks. I have ascertained that during their voyage home husband and wife quarreled.

"It was the present duke who got Madame Dulk sentenced to imprisonment for endeavouring to obtain money under false pretenses.

"She produced the child, but at the critical moment her husband went off with the documents necessary to establish its identity. In fact, it was the usual criminal bungle.

181

"But though the duke, for his own protection, sent this woman to gaol, he quite believed her tale, and when she was released, he had some other transaction with her, for she was then able to produce the documents she had so much wanted before.

"She and her husband had now come to some sort of agreement again.

"When the duke heard that rose had really been found again, he did not forbid this woman to secure her. He wavered between his good impulses and his bad ones.

"He had not made up his mind what to do about his niece, when his only son was struck down with awful suddenness. The duke has taken this catastrophe s a warning from above, and he has now resolved to freely recognize Lady Rose Fenton, and to accord her the revenues and privileges which are her due.

"So, if you please, we will hasten on to Hanover Square, and keep this appointment with Messsrs. Martindale and Co. Why, gentlemen, you don't look just as delighted as you should with my great news."

"It seems," said Mr. Briarton, "that if we recover Rose it will be but to lose her a once in the turmoil of fashionable life."

"A medical student can scarcely aspire to the hand of a duke's daughter," said Ernest, in a crestfallen way.

"I could have given her as much money as she could ever reasonably spend," muttered Frank Ellaby.

"Nonsense!" cried Sexton Blake. "If the young lady is worth troubling about at all she will be just as good, and as lovable, bearing a title as if she remained a simple miss.

"I can't understand how it is," the detective grumbled, "but I get more dismayed when I give people good news than when I have to them the bad. It is the detective's lot to always be received in the opposite way from that which he has a right to expect."

Shortly afterwards they left the house but did not go far in a westwardly direction. They were soon stopped by the hoarse cries of newspaper vendors, who were already board with the ghastly tiding of—

"SUIDICE OF THE DUKE OF FENTON!"

It was too true. The untimely cutting of his much-loved son had driven the nobleman to this rash act.

"We are as far from finding Rose as ever," groaned Mr. Briarton.

"I fear so," said Mr. Blake, "his lawyers know nothing at all concerning her whereabouts."

On their return to the hotel, Mr. Briarton was informed that a rough-looking man was waiting in the minister's sitting room to see him, and that he has some very important information for them.

They all went up, but it chanced that Frank Ellaby was the first to enter the apartment.

"What!" he cried, recognizing the burly figure standing

183

defiantly with his back to the window. "I'm glad I have you at last, Bill Bender!"

He would have made a spring on to his old gaoler, but Bill Bender seized a heavy cut-glass water bottle which was near at hand, and raising it high above his head, cried—

"Move a step, and I'll brain you!"

Sexton Blake, who had followed Frank in, caught the situation with half a glance.

He made a dart round through another room onto the balcony outside. Springing through the window of Mr. Briarton's room, he caught Bill from behind, and had him on the floor before that powerful gentleman was aware of his presence.

At the same moment Ernest Truelove sprang to the detective's help.

"Don't kill me!" gasped Bill, "you'll never forgive yourselves if you do. I've got a message—a message from the young lady—from Miss Rose Briarton!"

CHAPTER XII.

The Discovery of Rose—An Awful Tragedy—The End.

Leon Polti's amiable intention of delivering Rose up to the people of the Silver Bell Hotel, receiving the reward for her restoration and so baulking Madame Dulk's well-laid plans, would have taken very quick effect but for the fact that during his morning ramble through the ground he detected the form of Bill Bender skulking among the trees.

A feeling of cold terror struck him, for he knew well this desperate character had only one purpose in being there—it was to kill Leon. The latter was sure that so far Bill had not seen him—had, indeed, only guessed that he might be at this rendezvous. So he crept quickly back to the house, resolved to

185

remain in hiding until his enemy should grow tired of watching.

He had one consolation, and it was that while Bill lay waiting for them outside, Madame Dulk would not dare to venture out to set her schemes in motion either.

"It's a bitter reflection that I should be caged up here and powerless to denounce the murderer of my husband, when he might be so easily taken," declared that lady angrily.

"All might have gone well had we left this Frank Ellaby alone. The unlucky plot emanated from you and your husband. Now the hue and cry is out after us hot and active," said Leon.

"Bah! I have no fear of that. What can they prove against me?"

"Sufficient to send you into penal servitude for life. The sooner we are both out of the country the better."

"True. But you way shall not be my way. I have some little business to settle, and that accomplished I shall be able to take care of myself in future."

"That is exactly my case," muttered Leon to himself, "and both our interests revolve around that young girl."

Aloud he added, "So long as Bill remains on guard outside we are powerless to do anything."

"If you were a man, you would go out and kill him," said Madame contemptuously.

"And attract the attention of the police to this, our only remaining refuge? No, thanks, all we can do is to wait."

Polti was not the only one who had seen Bill Bender

lurking in those woods. Rose, at first, much to her alarm, had encountered him in one of her brief walks, and promising him rich rewards, had persuaded him to take her message to Mr. Briarton, at the Silver Bell Hotel. Bill had means of scaling the high walls which surrounded the grounds, but it was impossible for her to do so.

Bill's surprise at finding himself face to face with Frank Ellaby can well be imagined. It is not surprising that he blamed himself for having walked into a trap so simply laid for him.

"Now, look here," said the desperado, when they allowed him to regain his feet, though they had securely bound his hands. "If you want to rescue that young lady, I know where she is, and I will take you to her. But you'll have to let me go scot free afterwards. If you can't agree to those terms, my lips remained closed for ever, you may all perish before I'll give you any help."

"Remember, Bill," said Blake, "we are not the police, and we can't control them. Take us to where Miss Rose Briarton is confined, and we will give you your freedom right enough; but you will have to take your chance as to whether the police get you or not."

"That's a chance I take every day," growled the ruffian. "Come on, I'm your man. Not one of you must leave my sight. I'm not going to have you giving information. The place lies between Bedford and St. Neots. It don't take very long to get there!"

187

They reached their destination in due course.

As they stood in front of the park-like gates of the principal drive they opened, and Polti, closely muffed up, emerged into the high road. He was alone, and in a smart gig, to which was harnessed a strong, spirited horse.

At the sight of Bill he uttered a cry of dismay, and slashed the beast in front of him unmercifully.

But there was no escape for him!

With a roar like that of a tiger Bill sprang on to the back of the vehicle. By sheet muscular strength he dragged his heavy body up on to the seat by the side of the driver.

Here commenced a fierce and awful struggle for life!

The tugging and jerking of the reins, the swaying of the gig, the dreadful mutterings of the combatants, maddened the high-spirited horse.

Getting the bit between its teeth, it tore madly forward, blind to all before it!

"See!" cried Ernest, in a tone of horror, "where the road takes a sudden bend it skirts a cutting, which makes a sheer drop of forty feet into the turbulent stream. Will that excited animal hold to the highway, or go over?"

Not until the horse reached the edge of the cutting did it realize its danger. With a sudden jerk it turned, as if to get back to the highway and safety once more.

As if by a miracle, the sudden jerk caused the shafts to snap off short, and the traces, which held the horse, were torn in two. The animal retained its footing, but the gig and the two men, went over the awful height.

And still they struggled, though they were descending to their doom!

They disappeared down the deadly chasm into the deep, fast-running water!

When they were found it was seen that, in the descent, the gig had turned completely over, and had buried Leon and Bill under it at the bottom of the stream, so they had no chance of swimming for their lives, even if they were conscious when they reached the water.

This dreadful tragedy had been witnessed from one of the upper windows of the mansion by Madame Dulk. Except that the horror of it fascinated her for a moment, it occasioned her no regret. She turned away with a shrug of her shoulders.

The telegram she held in her hand concerned her more deeply. It told her of the suicide of the Duke of Fenton. It urged her to meet the sender of it at St. Neots that night.

It was signed "Belus."

"So the duke has gone," she murmured, "and with him my last hope of immediate wealth and safety. The documents proving the legitimacy of Rose are still in my possession, and should be valuable. But I dare not offer them to Frank Ellaby and to Mr. Briarton. It would be one more crime to the list they have against me.

"They had best be destroyed. They shall never benefit

189

any person but myself for I have gone through much to secure and retain them."

From her traveling bag she withdrew a packet of papers. In the act of casting them into the fire, she paused.

"Even yet they may be of service," she reflected.

At that moment she heard the voice of Frank Ellaby and the others, as they ascended the principal stairs.

"The end has come! They are here to take me!" she ejaculated in terror.

"But they shall never have these precious proofs."

The documents she had sinned so deeply to obtain she cast on to the burning coat, and the flames greedily devoured them.

The voices came nearer and nearer. They passed her room, and next she heard a joyous cry from Rose, as she was once again in the clergyman's embrace, and in the sunshine of her lover's glad welcome.

Quickly and silently Madame ran into her bedroom. Seizing her cloak and hat, and securing her valuables, she crept down the back staircase, out of the house on to the free, wide road.

She met Belus at St. Neots that evening. To her dismay he was accompanied by a couple of the London police inspectors, who very adroitly decorated her wrists with a pair of handcuffs, and conveyed her straight to the London train, which was already in the station, impatient to commence its rush to the

Metropolis.

The two officers from Scotland Yard informed her that they had secured sufficient evidence against her to warrant any judge in sending her to prison for fifteen years.

"When you in your fury threw that lamp at me, and burned half my body away, I swore to be revenged on you," cried Belus, thrusting his malicious, evil face into the carriage window.

"And my time has come now. Take her away, gentlemen—take her away to her righteous doom!"

With a scream of satisfaction the engine dashed forward, and was soon lost in the darkness of the night.

Frank Ellaby, being in doubt as to what he should do with his wealth, has showered most of it on Rose and Ernest, those fortunate young people who in a few months' time are to be made man and wife.

Sexton Blake has been well rewarded, and he and Mr. Gervaise, of Paris, are partners.

"I did the best I could for you in the matter," he once said to Ellaby; "but it was not so much as I wished."

"Thank goodness!" said the Rev. Fred Briarton, "we have been the means of suppressing those terrible people, the 'Red Lights of London.'"

"Yes," agreed Frank; "we have managed to clear away four desperate criminals at least."

THE END

Coming soon:

Lord Lister, known as Raffles Master Thief: The Great Unknown

Joseph A. Lovece is a retired journalist, and collector of dime novels, pulp magazines and comic books. He lives in Ormond Beach, Florida.

Made in the USA
Charleston, SC
10 February 2015